At Home in Old Sodus

ISBN: 978-0-9829756-0-2

Published by:
First School Press
P.O. Box 115
Sodus, Michigan 49126

Edited by Rachel Starr Thomson
Cover Design by Jay Cookingham

Printed in the United States of America

At Home in Old Sodus

by
Michael Leonard Jewell

To my dear wife Susan—
who has hastened on to heaven before me.
Thank you for staying after me to write.

To my parents—
Burton and Virginia Jewell.
Thank you for teaching me not to be helpless.

To the Lord Jesus Christ—
the ultimate Hero of this story
and my life.

Table of Contents

One

Sam Has a Secret

One chilly Saturday morning in late October, the ancient maples that lined the streets in the tiny village of Sodus dripped with heavy dew. The rising sun made them sparkle, and their few remaining leaves fluttered to the ground. Across from the coal yard by the railroad tracks was a narrow white house. Inside, Mary Bridges was setting the table for breakfast. Amberley was just coming down the stairs when she heard her father's loud voice in the kitchen. She paused on the last step and leaned against the banister to listen.

"Ramsey spouts like that all the time, Sam. He hasn't thrown us out yet."

"Ha! We used to be his only tenants, but maybe now he figures it might be good for business if he cracks down on us. Maybe his other renters will pay better if he makes us an example!"

Mary paused for a moment and then spoke softly. "Sam, is there something you're not telling me? What was in that registered letter you signed for yesterday?"

Sam reached for his coat.

"It was nothing! I've got to get going right away. I have a lead on a job, and I want to get there before someone else takes it. The man is new in town, and well, he doesn't know me yet. If I don't get there first to tell him what I can do, one of the boys will clue him in on what I can't."

"But Sam, you're the best carpenter in the township. I have never seen anyone's work with such skill and detail. Take the pictures of your work along to show him. Surely you will get the bid."

Mary's tender words of loyalty brought a brief smile to Sam's face, but his expression quickly changed to bitterness. "But would you want a drunkard carving your fine walnut cabinets? I haven't had a single bid in over a month. The rent is past due now! Would you hire someone who hasn't worked in over a month?"

"It'll work out, Sam. I know it will. Perhaps we can ask my mother for help."

"I said that we aren't going to the family or anyone else for charity. Now that's final!"

Amberley took a deep breath and barged into the kitchen, purposely dropping some books on the floor to announce her presence.

"Please, Sam," Mary hushed him. "Not in front of Amber."

Amberley was Sam and Mary's only child and had just

begun seventh grade. She had her mother's red hair and a few freckles on her cheeks. She also had her father's flaming blue eyes. She tried to smile, but the room went silent as she sat down to breakfast. Sam looked at his daughter and then at his wife. He turned, picked his hat off the hook, and went slamming out the door. Amberley wondered if he had already started drinking from the bottle he kept in his work shed. Mary glanced at her daughter and then quickly left the room. Amberley was left all alone in the strange silence. *Here we go again*, she thought, staring at the plates of steaming hot food.

About four o'clock that afternoon a knock sounded at the back door. It was Mrs. Enkins, the neighbor lady from across the alley. She stood in front of the glass holding a large cardboard box, covered with a yellow gingham towel, in her arms. Sylvia Enkins was short and petite, almost lost in her beautiful handmade apron. Her eyes barely peered over the top of the box she was carrying.

"Hello, honey! Tom came home from work and insisted that we go out for dinner. I had already cooked a pot roast with all the trimmin's. Would you be a dear and take it off my hands? I hate to waste food, and Tom isn't partial to leftovers."

Amberley could see that her mother's eyes were beginning to sparkle with tears.

"Sure, we'll be glad to help you out."

Mary carried the heavy box into the kitchen and threw

3

back the towel. The luscious smell caused their mouths to water. There was a large roast beef that must have weighed seven or eight pounds, all smothered with carrots and onions. There was buttery corn from Mrs. Enkins's summer garden, hot buttermilk biscuits, mashed potatoes, and beef gravy. Covered under a sheet of waxed paper lay a warm pumpkin pie with a dish of whipped cream.

"It'll last for several meals at least! Mrs. Enkins didn't make all of this food for just her and Tom. What a dear!"

Amberley smiled. She knew there hadn't been much money coming in lately for groceries, except when Ma occasionally did laundry and housekeeping for some of the neighbor ladies. After weeks of cornmeal mush, this feast would be an unexpected treat.

* * *

Dusk was falling upon Sodus, and the whistle from the evening train brought Amberley back to reality. She had been reading *A Girl of the Limberlost* and had spent the late afternoon collecting moths in the great Limberlost swamp. She quickly closed her book and hurried down the stairs.

Mary had just set the table for dinner and, as was her custom, lit a single candle on the window sill above the sink.

"Ma, have you heard from Dad yet? He's been gone all day," Amberley asked.

"Hush now, Amber! It takes time to work out the details of a bid. He'll be home soon."

Suddenly, the door banged open, and there stood Sam. His coat was wet from the cold rain that had started to fall, and the wind blew a few leaves across the floor. His eyes were red and his breathing was heavy. The beaten look of disappointment on his face said everything. He had been drinking. They could smell it.

Amberley knew they had no money, so she just assumed that one of her father's friends had treated him to a drink. She gritted her teeth in disgust. Her father's so-called friends were quick to undermine him when he was trying to find work, but just as quick to console him with a drink when he failed.

Sam paused to look at his wife and daughter and then turned to hang his hat and coat on the hook behind the door.

"Sit down to dinner, Sam. I've kept it warm in the oven." Mary pulled out his chair.

Sam sat down at his place at the table, and after a few moments of silence, he spoke.

"When I was in the Special Forces, I was responsible for the lives of my men and millions of dollars worth of equipment. I really did try to liberate the oppressed!" he cried out.

Amberley closed her eyes as her father referenced the Green Beret motto. She'd heard it so many times before

5

when he was like this.

"Now they won't hire me at the fruit exchange across the street!"

Amberley couldn't tell if there were tears in her father's eyes or if it was just the rain.

Mary set a large platter of the precious roast beef dinner on the table before Sam. He squinted his eyes, trying to understand what he was seeing.

"Where did you get that kind of food? Who gave you money?"

"Nobody gave me money, Sam. Mrs. Enkins made a big dinner for Tom. When he came home from work today, he wanted to take her out to eat. She asked me if we could take the food off her hands. Wasn't that nice of her, Sam?" Mary's face was a beaming smile.

Sam pushed the chair back from the table and stood up in a rage.

"I don't believe that, and neither do you. It's just some more of your church friends givin' us handouts. Well, we ain't no charity case. I can feed my own family. Take that food back right now or I'll . . . ! Amber! Go to your room!"

Amberley burst into tears and ran crying to her bedroom at the top of the stairs. She slammed the door. She could hear her mother pleading with Dad not to shame her in front of the neighbors, but he wouldn't listen when he was like this. Amberley tried to cover her ears with her hands, but she could not shut out the sound. She had been through this so many times before that her brain was swimming with emotion. At this very moment, she hated her father!

How could he be so mean to Ma and to nice Mrs. Enkins? How could he be so mean to me? she thought. *I know why Daddy can't find work. It's because the whole town knows he's a drunk! Nobody wants to hire a drunk! I hate Daddy, I hate him!*

She vented her hot fury into her pillow. She sobbed and sobbed, and soon her tears yielded to sleep as the overwhelming cares of her world faded away.

Two
Amberley Is an Unexpected Friend

It was very early morning when Amberley opened her eyes. She could scarcely believe that she had slept through the whole night. Her long red hair was tangled and stuck to her face from a runny nose and teardrops.

Amberley took a warm bath and put on her favorite blue dress—her only good dress. It was Sunday morning, and she and Ma would be walking to church.

As she thought about the night before, a wave of guilt and shame came over her for saying that she hated her father. She really loved him very much, but she hated it when he drank and argued with Ma. *I know that Daddy loves us very much,* she thought. *He just wants to provide good things for me and Ma.*

It was almost November and growing colder every day. Amberley gazed down the street from her window at the wet mountain of coal beside the train tracks. Raindrops struck the glass on her window like strokes from a paintbrush. She traced them with her finger until she realized that she had stalled long enough and had to go downstairs.

Amberley quietly entered the kitchen, soaking up its warmth and coziness. There was a good fire in the oil burner by the wall.

"Sit down to breakfast, Amber," Ma said.

Ma had made a breakfast of fried cornmeal mush and sorghum molasses. Amberley was famished! Her stomach growled, and the golden brown slices of fried mush were as tempting as beefsteak.

Sam was seated at the kitchen table and did not look up when Amberley found her place next to him. He sat quietly with his head down, poking at the food on his plate. Finally, after ten minutes of loaded silence, he put down his fork.

"Amber, honey," he said, still not looking up, "I'm very sorry about last night. I don't know what to say. I guess I never do. I'm sorry, and I . . ."

The remainder of his sentence trailed off as Amberley sat in silence, staring at her plate. Sam watched his daughter carefully and then glanced up at his wife, shrugging his shoulders in hopelessness. Perhaps this time he had gone too far in one of his drinking tirades. He resumed his brooding posture in front of his plate, pretending he did not expect a response from his daughter. But he wanted one so badly, and the silent moments were about to crush him.

Mary watched them both in pain. She wanted to tell

Amberley that her father was seeking a path back into her good graces, but she couldn't. The forgiveness must be genuine and arise from her daughter's own heart.

"I love you too, Daddy," Amberley said finally as her eyes began to moisten. She leaned over and kissed him on his unshaven cheek.

* * *

On the way home from church that morning, Amberley wondered how she might start a conversation with her father about coming to the services. It wasn't easy to talk to him, especially about spiritual matters. The rain from that morning had abated, and she and Ma kicked through the wet leaves on the sidewalk.

"Ma, did Daddy ever come to church with you—when you first got married, I mean?"

"Yes, for a while. Why do you ask?"

"I was thinking that if only we could get him to come to church, maybe he would stop drinking and find some new friends."

Ma smiled. "Sweetheart, I would love for your father to come to church with us. I have tried to get him to come every week since I can remember, but that would only be a start. It's not going to cure his drinking or any other problem."

Amberley was surprised. Surely by coming to church

10

her father would change his ways. He was really a good man at heart. He just needed to attend church on a regular basis.

Mary reached down and took her daughter's hand.

"Amber, every change for good in a person's life must first start with a personal relationship with the Lord. Your dad needs to first trust the Lord Jesus as his personal Savior. Coming to church or swearing off drink only amounts to turning over a new leaf. The change is on the surface, and temporary at best. Going to church doesn't make you a Christian any more than sleeping in the garage makes you a car. The change must start in the heart, when a man sees himself as a sinner and then calls on Christ to save him. Yes, your father is a good man, but he doesn't know the Lord."

Amberley was puzzled. She narrowed her eyes and turned to look at her mother.

"You see, I fell in love with your father when I was very young. He was so dashing and handsome in his green beret and uniform, but I knew he wasn't saved. I thought, like many women do, that I could change him. He promised me that he would get saved, and I believed him."

Amberley thought about the night that she had been saved. Pastor Mitchell had said that people don't go to hell because they are bad, but because they refuse to accept the remedy for their sins—Jesus Christ.

She decided that she would try to speak to her father

11

that afternoon after a good Sunday dinner. He had been in such a tender mood that morning and had spoken so sweetly to her that she felt surely she might be able to speak to him.

As Amberley and her mother walked home through the leaf-cluttered streets, they talked and were happy. They could hear the afternoon train coming from Benton Harbor, and Officer Moore, the part-time Sodus police officer, honked his horn and waved at them as he drove by. Ma was so cheerful that Amberley was sure her parents had made up. Mrs. Enkins had paid Ma for some washing she had done on Friday, so there was money for a good Sunday dinner of meatloaf and baked potatoes.

"Ma, why does Mrs. Enkins pay you to do her laundry? I was in her house last week, and she has a brand new washer and dryer."

"Mrs. Enkins says that her arthritis bothers her something fierce on wash day," Ma answered.

"But Ma, she works in her garden and knits and sews just fine. Remember the beautiful hand-sewn quilt she entered in the county youth fair? The patterns were sewn with such detail."

Ma stopped and touched her daughter's arm.

"Amber, I want you to keep a secret just between us girls. Mrs. Enkins is just pretending to have bad arthritis. She knows how bad times are for us, and this is her way of helping. If your father ever found out, he would blow his stack."

"Why doesn't Daddy want to ask Grandma Andrews for help? She has lots of money."

"Because it's charity, and he's a proud man. His father was the same way. Grandma would love to help us, but your father would find out. He doesn't mind Mrs. Enkins's money because I'm working for it. If he found out what she was doing, well, it would be Saturday night in Sioux City!"

As they walked down the alley to their house, they noticed that the back door was wide open. The color in Ma's face drained away as she ran up the steps and into the house.

"Sam? Sam?" she shouted.

Amberley called out, "Daddy! Where are you?"

On the kitchen table lay a sheet of paper and an opened envelope. It was the registered letter Sam had signed for on Friday. Ma snatched the paper up off the table, read it through once, and then dropped into a chair.

Amberley knew that something was terribly wrong. She knew that she shouldn't ask right then, but she couldn't help herself. "Ma, what is it?"

Ma looked at the paper as if it were poisoned. After a moment of silence and a shake of her head, she turned to Amberley and contemplated her daughter's face.

"I guess that after all you've been through, you're no child anymore. You're my daughter, Amber, but right now I need a friend more. After all these years of Ramsey

13

threatening to evict us, he finally made good on his promise. He's going to sell our house right out from under us. This letter from the sheriff says that we must move out. Dad can't get work, and we can't pay the rent anymore. Ramsey is within his rights. The sheriff will be here in less than four weeks to evict us if we're not gone."

Amberley felt the thrill of nausea in her stomach. Her whole world seemed to be falling apart in an instant. Just a few moments ago they had been so happy. Amberley had wanted to speak to Dad that afternoon about the Lord, but now that notion seemed an impossible one.

Stop it! she said to herself. *I must be there for Ma!*

Ma sat crumpled at the table with her face in her hands. She looked so pitiful, and Amberley wondered if this might finally be Ma's breaking point.

Amberley arose silently from her chair and stood behind her mother. She put her arms around her neck and rested her chin against Ma's sweet-smelling red hair.

Then she thought, *Where's Daddy?*

But she didn't have to ask, because she already knew. He was doing what he always did when trouble came. He was out getting drunk.

Three
Steady On the Beam

That night, Amberley went quietly to her bed, tired and alone. She felt so helpless, as if the Lord had left her to handle all of her problems by herself. She laid her head on her pillow, and as she stared at the ceiling, tears began to flow down her cheeks. Even her mother couldn't help her now—Ma was worried about Dad and losing their home. Amberley's stomach felt like a swarm of bees.

The October wind blew hard against the house, and soon cold rain pattered her window. Her father was out there somewhere, and she didn't know if he would even come back.

She had read in her history book about the sad Depression time of the 1920s and '30s. Some of the men who couldn't find jobs took their own lives. She fought down her fears. Men had to work and support their families. God had put it inside them to do it. But her father was like those men in the 1920s—failing and hopeless.

Amberley could hear her mother coming up the stairs, so she sat up and quickly wiped her eyes. Ma stood at the door and tried to smile.

"What is it, Ma?"

"I was just thinking that perhaps we need to have our devotions together before we go to sleep. It's important for us to keep steady on the beam, even though our hearts may be breaking. God is still on His throne, and the Bible is still true, even when one loses his home. This isn't the time for us to go into a tailspin, and I guess I need to remind you and especially myself of that."

Ma sat down on the bed next to her daughter and opened her Bible.

"Amber, I want you to understand that when the unsaved world runs into trouble, they have no one to go to for help. There is no place of rest or comfort for them. That's why the Bible says 'the wicked are like the troubled sea, when it cannot rest.' As Christians, we have God as our great Resource. We have hundreds of verses of truth to draw upon for comfort and help. I don't think your father and I would still be married if it wasn't for the great comfort of God's Word and the privilege of prayer."

Ma showed Amberley the verse she had written on the inside of her old worn-out Bible many years ago.

"My favorite verse," she said.

Amberley read the verse out loud. "Psalm 37:25: 'I have been young, and now am old; yet have I not seen the righteous forsaken, nor His seed begging bread.'"

After they prayed together, Ma kissed Amber on the

forehead and quietly descended the stairs.

Amberley slipped out of her warm covers and knelt beside her bed. "Dear Lord Jesus, I know that I am just a poor girl, but I love You so much. You said that You would never forsake us and would not let us go hungry. We are not beggars, but we are Your children, the children of a great King. The sheriff will be here in a few weeks to make us leave our home, and now Daddy is out getting drunk. Please help us, Lord Jesus! Please help Daddy find work so we can find a new home, and most of all, please help Daddy to get saved. In Jesus' name, amen."

Amberley wiped the tears from her eyes with the sleeve of her flannel nightgown. She felt so much better and was sure that the Lord had heard her prayer. Sometimes, when she felt particularly lonely, she would pretend that the Lord Jesus was holding her in His big strong arms. That night He did hold her close as she drifted away into a deep sleep.

* * *

Monday morning was school. Amberley came down the cold stairs. She could see her breath, and she hurried to get into the warm kitchen. They were out of fuel oil again. Ma had hung a blanket over the doorway of the kitchen to keep in the heat. She had boiled water on the stove and left the oven door open to make it steamy warm. The room was cozy in spite of the rest of the house.

Ma fried up the leftover oatmeal and raisins for breakfast. She toasted bread in the oven and buttered it with the last of the butter.

Amberley thought, *What will happen when the food is all gone?* Then she thought again, *"Nor His seed begging bread."* Somehow the Lord would feed them.

After breakfast, Amberley helped her mother wash and dry the few dishes.

"Amber, would you like me to brush your hair?" Ma asked.

"Ma," Amberley said with a surprised laugh, "I'm twelve years old!"

"I know, but it seems like you're growing up so fast. I miss all the mornings I brushed your hair before you went off to school. I guess it was just a thought."

Her mother almost sounded as if she was talking to herself rather than to her daughter. Amberley's parents had lived in this house when they were first married and Sam was still in Vietnam. Amberley had grown up here. It was the only house she had ever known. She thought of the wonderful meals they had eaten together in the cozy kitchen with the bright yellow walls. Even with all their troubles, there had been many happy times.

"Ma, did Daddy come home last night?"

"Yes, dear. He is already out looking for work."

Amberley didn't ask if he had been drinking. She

didn't want to know. She was just thankful that he was all right.

"That's good, Ma."

Amberley kissed her mother good-bye and waved out of habit as she walked the half-mile or so to Sodus School. As she passed McGuigan Street and the library, she was so absorbed in thought that she almost walked beyond the school to Chapel Hill. She caught herself and waited outside the school door, but she didn't even hear the bell ring. One of the Taylor twins touched her arm and brought her back to reality.

"Hey, kid, the earth's down here," Vickie Taylor laughed.

Amberley blushed but thanked her quietly. She would have been more embarrassed if she had walked in late for school.

During class, she was again so deep in thought that she failed to hear a question from the teacher, Mrs. Charin. This brought a round of snickers from the other students, and Teacher asked to see her after class.

When the classroom had emptied out and Amberley stood before Mrs. Charin's desk, the kindly teacher asked, "What is it, dear? You've been in another world since you came to school today."

Mrs. Charin was a member of Amberley's church and a caring friend. Her sweetness and presence seemed to bring warmth to the worldly coldness of the classroom.

Amberley explained all about her father and the letter.

Mrs. Charin leaned forward in her chair and put her pencil in her hair. "I am so sorry, sweetie, but I want you to remember something. As a Christian, you can be assured that God knew this was going to happen in your life. This may not seem very comforting when you are about to lose your home, but remember Romans 8:28: 'All things work together for good.' Think of this verse as being like an umbrella. As long as you stay under it, all things will work together for good according to His purpose. It has not been easy for me to teach in a public school, but I get through knowing that the Lord is in charge and only wants what is best for me. Somehow, dear, this thing will work out for you and your folks. Now, let's ask the Lord to help get you through it. "

Amberley and Mrs. Charin bowed their heads in the silence of the classroom and asked the Lord to take charge of the situation.

". . . and dear Lord, please help Mr. Bridges to find work and please show him his need of the Savior. In Jesus' name, amen."

Amberley walked home alone. The other students were long gone, and the street was quiet and empty. She thought about what Mrs. Charin had said. Somehow she had to let go and let the Lord handle this crisis. How very black it all seemed. She wasn't as good a Christian as her mother and Mrs. Charin, and she was tempted to pick up the burden she had just laid down at God's feet. All she had was her salvation and the promises from the Bible. That would have to be enough.

Four

God Answers Big Prayers

The four weeks passed quickly. It was Thursday afternoon, and when Amberley came home from school, there were boxes stacked all over the front room. The manager of the IGA store on the corner next to the old fire station had given Ma all of his old boxes. She had been packing all day and looked so tired. Her hair was disheveled, and despite the cold, her face was damp with perspiration.

"I have just a few more things to pack, honey, and then I must contrive a cold supper before your father gets home. He's checking on a maintenance job at the pickle factory in Hipps Hollow, but I don't know if he'll get it. I— we—must be ready for whatever happens." Ma didn't look up as she spoke.

Amberley walked upstairs and found all of her things packed away in boxes. Only her bedding was left intact. Her old doll Jenny lay on her pillow next to her Bible. She reached for Jenny, but picked up her Bible instead and sat on the floor, seemingly in a trance. She held the book close to her as if its very presence would change the situation.

The room was cold, and she could see her breath. She closed her eyes and was only brought back to reality when she heard her mother coming up the stairs.

"Don't start crying, honey. I don't want your eyelids to freeze." Ma smiled wryly as she sat down beside her daughter.

Amberley looked at her mother and smiled. "Ma? I don't think I could ever cry another drop. Why didn't you wait and let me help you with the packing?"

"Because I wanted to keep everything like a home as long as I could. I didn't want us to sit around for days staring at boxes."

Ma put her arm around Amberley's waist. "I know what you mean about the crying. I cried my last tear this morning, and as you can see, it hasn't helped our situation a bit."

"What time tomorrow will the sheriff be here, Ma?"

"In the morning, sweetheart. The sheriff will be here in the morning."

Amberley had been avoiding the details of their plight, hoping it would all go away. But now she wanted to know everything. "What will happen to us, Ma?"

"Well, you and I will go to live with Grandma Andrews on the farm, and your father . . ." Ma hesitated. "Your father will go to live at the rescue mission in Benton Harbor."

Amberley felt sick to her stomach. She knew about that place. It was full of dirty, smelly men who couldn't stop drinking liquor. Sometimes they didn't come out of there alive. Amberley inhaled a deep breath as a pang of sorrow gripped her heart. "Is Daddy going there because he's a drunk?"

"Amber! Don't say such things about your father," Ma said sternly. "He needs to be where he can find work so we can be together again. Pastor Mitchell suggested it, and, well, maybe they can help your father, too. It will only be for a little while. Now come downstairs before you catch cold."

That night they sat in the warm kitchen together, perhaps for the last time. They had finished their supper of cold tomato sandwiches, and Dad stood at the window, peering out into the dark alley. Ma said nothing as she busied herself darning one of Dad's socks. Amberley tried to read her book about the Limberlost, but she couldn't concentrate. The moths and the swamp would have to wait for happier days.

She put her book down and watched the kettle boil on the hot stove, pretending it was the smokestack of a big steamship. She thought how happy the passengers must be. She wished that her family could get on a big ship right now and sail around the world. That way they could all stay together always. She thought about how King David had said, "Oh that I had wings like a dove! For then would

I fly away, and be at rest."

Dad broke the silence with his deep voice. He began slowly.

"Girls, this will be our last night together as a family for awhile. I'm afraid that I have been a rotten husband and father."

"No, Daddy, no!" Amberley said.

"Please, Sam, don't," Ma pleaded.

"It's true, girls. I have tried to do everything my way, and it has always fallen through. They taught us in the Forces to take care of ourselves and not to count on anyone else for help. That is how I've lived my life. I thought that God and church were for the weak. I have always detested weakness. But now I know that I *am* weak, and for the first time in my life, I see that I need God. I've been running from Him my whole life but wouldn't admit it."

Dad turned and looked into Ma's eyes. Amberley could not speak, but her heart fluttered with expectation.

"Mary, I made a promise to you over twelve years ago that I would get saved, but I kept putting it off. It seemed there was always a more convenient time to deal with God and eternity. The longer I stalled, the harder my heart became, and the more embarrassed I was. The truth is that I have started every day in terror, knowing that if I died I would be in hell before sunset. I made you girls suffer with my drinking and my foul mouth. Now God has taken everything away from me, including my family. We may be apart for a long while, but I can't bear the thought of being apart from you forever. Mary, if you will show me how, I would like to get saved if it's not too late."

Amberley almost fell off her chair, and tears began to fall from Ma's eyes. This is what they had been waiting and praying for all this time. Amberley could only say, "Oh, Daddy!"

Ma asked Amberley to get her Bible from the table in the front room.

"Sam, I'm going to take you through a few verses to show you the plan of salvation from the Book of Romans," Ma explained.

She took her Bible from Amberley and carefully read Romans 3:23: "'For all have sinned, and come short of the glory of God.' Sam, you have already admitted to us that you are a sinner and need God, but you must admit it to Him also. Before you can do business with God, you must first acknowledge that you are a sinner."

Ma read another verse—Romans 6:23: "For the wages of sin is death; but the gift of God is eternal life through Jesus Christ our Lord."

Ma laid a hand on her husband's shoulder. "Sam, there is a penalty for our sin, and that is death. Not just the kind of death when our bodies die, but an eternal death and separation from God forever in the Lake of Fire. But Romans 5:8 says, 'But God commendeth his love toward us, in that, while we were yet sinners, Christ died for us.' Sam, because the Lord Jesus died in our place, God offers us eternal salvation as a free gift if we will only accept it."

Ma's hands were shaking, and she could barely read the last verse through her tears. Amberley sat quietly, praying for her father.

"Finally, Sam, you must ask the Lord Jesus to save you." Ma read Romans 10:13: "For whosoever shall call upon the name of the Lord shall be saved."

They were quiet for a moment, then Ma blinked back a few tears and smiled. "It's that easy, Sam."

Dad spoke softly. "That is easy. Almost too easy."

"No, Sam. It was made easy for us, but it was not easy for God. He gave the most precious thing He had—His only begotten Son. The Lord Jesus went willingly to the cross to die for us so we could have eternal life. Would you like to pray now and ask the Lord to save you?"

Dad was silent. Amberley held her breath. Ma earnestly looked into her husband's eyes.

At last, Dad nodded. He knelt down next to the kitchen table and cleared his throat. "Dear Lord, I have been running for a long time. I know I'm a sinner and deserve to go to hell. I know you died for me, and I ask you to forgive my sins and save me. Amen."

Amberley's breath caught! *Did Daddy really mean it?*

Ma sobbed once with joy. "Did you mean that, Sam? Did you really mean that?"

"Yes, Mary, with all my heart I did."

Ma stood up from the table and put her arms around Dad. They held each other for a long time. Amberley almost felt like she was intruding until Dad motioned for her to come to him also. They all wept together with joy and relief.

Amberley watched her big dad get up off his knees and walk to the cupboard over the sink. He opened the door and revealed a full bottle of whiskey.

"I was saving this to get drunk on tomorrow after the sheriff left. I guess I won't need it now."

Dad opened the bottle and poured the contents down the drain. Amberley heard Ma whisper under her breath.

"Thank you, Lord."

That said it all.

Five

Unexpected

Sam and Mary didn't sleep very well that night as they lay on the front room floor amidst a forest of boxes. Amberley tried to sleep upstairs in her little room, but she finally took her blanket and cuddled up next to Mary. They were awakened early in the morning by the sound of Sam banging the coffee pot on the stove.

"Is it time, Ma?" Amberley said softly, almost in her mother's ear.

"Let's get up, dear," Mary whispered as they folded up the remaining bedding and put it in a waiting box.

Sam had borrowed a truck to move their things to Grandma Andrews's farm. He finished a cup of coffee reheated from the night before as he waited for enough daylight to start moving boxes and furniture out into the alley. Mary toasted some leftover biscuits in the oven, and the heat made the kitchen feel good. Amberley ate one with a dab of Mrs. Enkins's strawberry jam.

At just past eight o'clock there came a loud banging at the back door. It was Sheriff Warner and a deputy.

Amberley's stomach beehive returned in full force. She breathed a short prayer. *Dear Lord Jesus, please help us to trust in You!*

Sheriff Warner was not a mean man, and he greeted Sam and Mary with a cordial handshake. "I'm sorry," he said. "I'm only doing my job. This is one of the hardest things about being sheriff." He motioned to his deputy to give a hand as he said, "Now, Mr. Bridges, how can we help?"

"I guess we can start in the front room," Sam said as he bent down to pick up a box.

As the men repeated trip after trip to the alley, Mary and Amberley could see Mr. and Mrs. Enkins come puffing up the path.

"What's going on here, Sam?" said Mr. Enkins sternly.

Sam was surprised to see Mr. Enkins. He tried to hide his shame and humiliation by taking him aside to tell him that he was being evicted. As soon as Mr. Enkins heard it, he brushed Sam aside and hurried up to the sheriff. He was almost comical, wearing his house slippers and letting one of the straps from his bib overalls drag on the ground.

"See here, sheriff, why are you evicting these good people from their home?" Mr. Enkins said, pointing his finger at the sheriff.

The sheriff put down the heavy box he was carrying. "I have no choice, sir. The owner swore out an eviction notice. It's all legal."

"Sheriff, it could not be legal! I know the owner of this house personally, and he could not have sworn out a notice!"

Sam handed the eviction papers to Mr. Enkins. "It's all right here, Mr. Enkins. I'm afraid it's all true."

Mr. Enkins unfolded the papers and held them at arm's length, trying to read the small print. Mrs. Enkins, who was standing nearby, handed him his glasses.

"Sheriff, do you realize that these documents are over thirty days old?"

"So?" the sheriff said curtly.

Mr. Enkins handed the papers to the sheriff and said, "Sheriff, I happen to know that these documents are incorrect!"

Sheriff Warner glanced at his deputy with a sarcastic smile and said, "Oh yeah, well, just how do you know that? I don't want to be unkind, sir, but this is really none of your business."

Mr. Enkins took some folded papers from his shirt pocket and handed them to the sheriff. The sheriff unfolded them and slowly read and reread the several pages of the document.

"Well, I'll be." He looked at Mr. and Mrs. Enkins and said, "Is this true? This is the way you want it?"

Mr. Enkins smiled. "Yes, sheriff, this is exactly the way we want it."

Sheriff Warner shook his head and began to chuckle.

"Well, I've certainly seen everything."

The frowning deputy reached for the papers to read them for himself. "What do they say, sir?"

The sheriff stooped down and picked up the box again. "It says that we need to carry all of this stuff back into the house."

The deputy scratched his head while the Bridges family stood with curious looks on their faces. It was clear that they didn't understand.

"Apparently," Sheriff Warner explained, nodding in the direction of the Mr. and Mrs. Enkins, "these folks here have just bought this house from a Mr. Bill Ramsey. They are the owners now, and they have a rental agreement all drawn up, ready for you folks to sign. They own the place, lock, stock, and barrel, and they want you folks to stay."

The shock could be read on their faces. God had answered their prayers in a way that they had never expected. Mr. and Mrs. Enkins were their new landlords!

As they hurried to put the boxes back into the house, a fuel oil truck pulled up into the alley. Mr. Enkins told the driver to "Fill 'er up."

"I can't have the pipes freezing in my house," he said to Sam with a wink.

Sam's expression showed a mix of relief and embarrassment. "See here, Mr. Enkins, I still can't pay the rent, whoever owns the house. And I won't be taking charity!"

"You won't be, Sam. Come and see me Monday morning. I checked up on you and found out you're a very good mechanic. A former Green Beret is just the kind of man I need to be foreman on my construction crew. I'll give you a chance to prove that you are that man."

Sam was stunned. "But Mr. Enkins . . . !" Mary threw her arms around her husband and gave him a hug and kiss before he could say anything else. She turned and thanked their neighbors for all they had done. Amberley thought of what Job had said: *Though He slay me, yet will I trust in Him.*

Sam called out to Mr. Enkins as he walked back down the alley.

"Mr. Enkins, you have just hired yourself the best foreman you've ever had!"

Six

Amberley Finds She Has a New Teacher

The future brightened considerably with Mr. and Mrs. Enkins as their landlords. Mr. Enkins told Sam that he felt their rent payment was too high because the house needed a lot of repairs. He promptly adjusted it down to a more reasonable amount and then paid Sam, as his employee, to do the much-needed repairs that had been neglected for years.

The weeks that passed with Sam working steadily allowed the Bridges family to begin getting back on their feet. The grocery bill at the IGA was soon paid in full, and they were able to open an account at the bank. They even had a telephone installed.

Christmas soon arrived, and Amberley received some badly needed school clothes. Sylvia Enkins invited the family over on Christmas Day for a wonderful dinner and a nice, relaxing afternoon. After apple pie and ice cream, Tom Enkins handed Sam a box wrapped in silver Christmas paper. Sam, who had never been able to accept gifts easily, sat speechless.

"Go ahead and open it, Dad," Amberley said.

Sam slowly and self-consciously opened the box, and there was a brand new King James Bible with the name "Sam Bridges" embossed in gold on a plain black cover. He solemnly thanked his new boss for the splendid gift. Amberley didn't think it was possible for two people to be as kind as Mr. and Mrs. Enkins were.

* * *

The holidays were almost over, and Amberley looked forward to returning to school the next day. It had been the best Christmas ever. Amberley sat in her room on the edge of her bed. She looked at her books and her blue wicker desk. It was her very own room. Someday she knew she must leave it, but not today.

Dad was much happier and more contented since he had gotten saved. He realized how much of his life he had wasted and was determined not to waste any more. He hadn't had a drink of liquor since that night, and his old drinking buddies couldn't believe that Sam Bridges had "got religion." They teased him when he came to town and even sent him a bottle of whiskey for Christmas as a joke. He just smiled and took the bottle outside to the tool shed. Ma and Amberley nervously watched him between the part in the curtain. He took a claw hammer off the shelf and broke the bottle over the ash can by the alley. Then he glanced back over his shoulder at them with a saucy grin.

Amberley had to get accustomed to walking to church with both her parents. There was a completeness in their family that had never been there before. When her dad went forward in church to make his salvation public, Pastor Mitchell announced that he looked forward to baptizing him just as soon as Pipestone Creek warmed up in the late spring.

The construction business was slow now because of the weather, and Ma was a little concerned that Dad might be laid off. Then one day, Mr. Enkins asked Dad to work with him all winter long, getting his equipment in shape for the next season. Amberley and Ma were so happy when Dad told them the good news. He had never been able to work year-round before.

It was bitterly cold the next morning, and Amberley wished she didn't have to walk. It was only a half-mile to Sodus School, but the blustering wind would make the trip seem like forever.

Ma had prepared a hot breakfast. She set on a bowl of grits and sausage gravy and the usual pan of golden hot biscuits. The kitchen was so warm and cozy that Amberley dreaded the thought of opening the back door.

They heard a car horn outside in the alley—it was time for Dad to leave for work. He rode in every morning with Mr. Enkins to his shop in Eau Claire. Dad put on his new heavy green coat made of cotton duck. It was a gift from

Mr. Enkins.

"Did you tell Mr. Enkins that you couldn't accept the new coat, Sam?" Ma teased.

"No, it's too cold out there," Dad chuckled. "Mary, I've been figuring, and perhaps by late spring we can buy a used car or pickup."

"Oh, that would be wonderful, Sam. We've never had a car before." Ma kissed him on the cheek.

The cold wind slapped at Amberley's face when she opened the door to leave for school. She had wrapped her scarf around her nose and mouth, but the cold still tried to come in. She knew Ma was watching her from the front-porch window as she made her way down the snowy street. She could hardly open her eyes to see where she was going, and once she tripped over the snow-covered railroad tracks.

As she stumbled through the wall of white, she could barely make out the other children walking to school. The bell rang as she entered the door, and the sudden warmth brought tears to her eyes and made her feet ache.

Amberley peeled the scarf from her face as the frost from her breath crackled off and fell to the floor of the cloakroom. She hung her coat on the hook and put her brown lunch bag on the shelf just above it. As she cheerfully entered the classroom to greet Mrs. Charin, the smile instantly fell from her face.

Standing behind Mrs. Charin's desk was a tall, thin woman with black hair and black, thick-rimmed glasses.

She appeared to be about the same age as Ma. She looked at Amberley with a stern unemotional expression and did not smile as Mrs. Charin always had.

The last bell rang, and all of the students hurried to reach their seats as the sound faded away. Everyone was so still that Amberley could hear her shoes squeak when she wiggled her toes. The new teacher tapped her desk smartly with a wooden pointer. "Attention! Attention, class! There will be no more talking. I am Miss Collins. I will be your new teacher."

One of the boys on the front row, Herbie Johnson, called out, "But where is Mrs. Charin?"

Miss Collins frowned and replied, "You will not blurt out questions, and you will raise your hand. I do not know where your former teacher is, and neither do I care. That is her business and not yours or mine."

There was an instant hush over the whole class. Sweet Mrs. Charin was no longer their teacher, and Miss Collins was. And she was mean, too! How could they make it through the school year?

Amberley had always enjoyed talking with Mrs. Charin at recess and lunchtime. They would often talk about the Lord, and Mrs. Charin seemed to genuinely care about Amberley and her problems. But now she had a new teacher who seemed to enjoy being mean to her students. This was going to be a long day—and a very long semester.

At noon hour, some of the students huddled together

to discuss the new teacher.

"She's like a drill sergeant!" Amberley said firmly.

"What is a drill sergeant?" Kathy Moore asked, twirling her long brown curls with her finger. Her father was the Sodus police officer.

"Well, I'm not exactly sure, but I know they are loud and mean. My dad says so." Amberley looked over her shoulder, feeling a little guilty that she was talking about Teacher behind her back.

She and Ma had often laughed out loud as Dad imitated the gruff voices of his drill sergeants. But Amberley was not laughing now, and when the bell rang to start science class that afternoon, she wished she was still on Christmas break.

Miss Collins adjusted her glasses, and with the wooden pointer in her hand, she tapped her desk again to bring the class to order. Herbie Johnson sat with his hands folded and his usual cheerful grin on his round face. Miss Collins pointed to Herbie with her wooden pointer.

"What is your name? Quickly now. What is your name?"

The smile left Herbie's face as he stammered for an answer. "Herb-Herbie, ma'am!" he said.

"Herbie, is it? Well, Herbert, you will remove yourself instantly from this room and stand in the hall for punishment. After class perhaps you can explain why you were laughing at the teacher."

Miss Collins's face was red as she struck her heavy wooden desk with the pointer. Amberley winced, startled by the loud noise. Herbie tried to explain to the teacher that he hadn't been laughing at her, but to no avail.

"Young man, you will please remove yourself at once to the hallway for punishment!"

Herbie slowly left his desk with a look of bewilderment and humiliation playing on his face. Amberley choked down her indignation. This new teacher didn't know Herbie as Mrs. Charin had. It was normal for him to flash his big toothy smile. That was just Herbie being Herbie.

Miss Collins took a deep breath and adjusted her heavy-rimmed glasses.

"We will open our science books to Chapter Ten. I see that this class is grossly behind in its studies. We must be diligent and move ahead to catch up. I will not tolerate a class that falls behind. Your former teacher was negligent in that respect."

Amberley felt her face grow warm. Miss Collins had no right to say those things against Mrs. Charin. Amberley didn't want to hear this new teacher anymore. She had been unkind to Herbie and insulting to Mrs. Charin. She wished she could speak with Ma right now to help her sort this out. Of course, Ma would tell her to be kind. But how could she be expected to be kind to this new teacher when she was so mean?

Seven
Amberley Tries To Cooperate

As the cold January wind blew Amberley home from school that afternoon, Ma was peeling potatoes at the sink.

"Can I help you, Ma?" Amberley asked, setting her books on the table and unwinding her long woolen scarf.

"All done, sweetheart."

"Ma, did you know that Mrs. Charin isn't teaching at Sodus School anymore?"

"Yes, I think I heard her mention it at church, but she didn't give a reason. I thought perhaps you knew."

Amberley sat at the kitchen table as Ma put the potatoes on to boil. She let out a sigh and rested her head against her pile of books.

"What is it, dear?" Ma asked. "I know how much you like Mrs. Charin."

"Oh Ma, this Miss Collins is such a horrible person!" Amberley almost wailed. "She sent Herbie to the hallway to punish him for no reason, and she said bad things about Mrs. Charin. I can't stand her! She's so mean, and I . . . I just

41

can't stand her!"

Amberley hugged her pile of books and began to sob until Ma brought her back to reality, sitting down in front of her with a concerned frown.

"Amber! You know better than that, and you have certainly been taught better!" Ma smoothed back Amberley's long red hair from her face. "Now, you sit up straight and tell me all about it!"

Amberley told her everything that had happened, and Ma couldn't help smiling a bit.

"You know, Amber, I wasn't much older than you when I lost my favorite teacher. Yes, dear; one moment it was sweet, kind Miss Ross, and a week later it was stern old Mr. Shelton. He would keep the older, incorrigible boys in line with a piece of rubber hose that he had in his desk. We all thought we were going to die."

Ma chuckled. "But it wasn't so bad. Mr. Shelton was a brilliant scholar, and we became very fond of him. I learned my Greek and Latin roots from him."

Amberley wiped her eyes and laid her head against Ma's arm. Ma spoke softly. "Let me tell you a secret. Promise you won't tell any of the other students?"

Amberley looked up into her mother's eyes. "I promise, Ma."

"Sometimes a new teacher, especially a very young teacher without a lot of experience, is frightened—just as you are when you start a new class. The teacher is unsure of her abilities and feels she must take control harshly to maintain order. Perhaps Miss Collins is a bit nervous and afraid, do you think?"

Ma smiled. "You know that the Lord would want you to be kind and supportive of your new teacher. Mrs. Charin would want that too. Why don't you give Miss Collins a chance and let her get comfortable with her new surroundings? Obey her, and help her to adjust as well as you can."

Ma smiled at her daughter and kissed her forehead. "Now come, help me get dinner on the table. These potatoes have to be mashed, and your father will be coming through that door any minute now."

Amberley rose from the chair and gathered her books in her arms. "You're right, Ma. I'll do my best."

* * *

The sun shone brightly the next morning, giving a false hope of warmth. The air was bitter, and a white mist hung closely to the ground. Hoar-frost formed on everything, and the snow squeaked under Amberley's feet.

The walk to school was almost intolerable in the extreme cold. Amberley wondered why they had to have school in the wintertime anyway. The bell rang as she approached the door, piled high with snow and ice like the entrance to an igloo.

She also wondered how she would hold up today. Everything had seemed so right and practical last night after talking to Ma in the warm glow of the kitchen. During her devotions that morning after breakfast, Amberley had prayed very hard that the Holy Spirit would guide her through this crisis. She really wanted to be a good student and not cause her new teacher any problems. But now, as she hung up her coat and slipped into her desk, she felt as if a shadow had come over her. Amberley knew that reading the Bible and praying in the comfort and security of her bedroom was fairly easy. Going into the cold world and putting it all into practice—that can be hard.

Miss Collins called class into session with the same abruptness as the day before. Herbie Johnson was back at his desk, but the usual grin was gone from his face.

Miss Collins taught them math, English, and history that morning and then gave them a short period to study. Amberley watched Miss Collins out of the corner of her eye. She was really rather pretty. She kept twirling her hair with her finger as she repeatedly glanced up at the ticking clock.

Suddenly, the silence was shattered when Miss Collins accidentally knocked a cup full of pencils onto the floor. Her face turned red. She froze as if she didn't quite know what to do next. Several of the boys scrambled to pick the pencils up. Miss Collins seemed to be in shock, disoriented as if, for a moment, she had shown her feet of clay. But a few snickers from the back of the room quickly brought her back to reality.

"Attention, class! Attention! There is no need to be making sounds. You will put your books away in preparation for lunch hour."

The bell rang for lunch, and at Teacher's dismissal, the students filed out the door to get their lunches from the cloakroom. Amberley stole a glance back. Miss Collins was sitting at her desk, leaning forward on both elbows with her face in her hands. She had removed her thick-rimmed glasses and was rubbing her eyes. She looked up for a moment, and she and Amberley made eye contact. Almost instantly, Miss Collins put on her glasses and resumed her former sternness. She straightened a few papers on her desk as Amberley left the room to get her plain brown lunch bag. She walked quietly back to her desk and tried not to look toward Miss Collins.

So Ma was right, she thought. *Teacher* is *frightened. Miss Collins must feel as if she doesn't have a friend in the world right now.* She breathed a short prayer and promised the Lord that she would try to be a help to her new teacher.

That afternoon, Miss Collins called the class to attention and told them to get out their science books.

"Chapter Eleven, please," she said, tapping her wooden pointer on her desk.

"We will be learning today about the origin of life and the evolution of man. The earth and the universe, as you should know, are billions of years old. We are not sure just exactly how it all started, but learned scientists tell us that a cloud of hot gases exploded and expanded into what is now the stars and our solar system."

Miss Collins paced back and forth in front of the gray slate chalkboard. "The earth was formed about five billion years ago. It became covered with great oceans and seas. Out of this formed the organisms that are the basis of all life on our planet. All life came from the oceans and evolved over millions of years into the plants and animals we have today. Modern man evolved over hundreds of thousands of years from extinct, ape-like animals."

Amberley was shocked! What she was hearing could not be true. Pastor Mitchell had taught them that the earth was only about six thousand years old and that the Lord had created everything that now exists in six days. Man was not an animal, but a special creation of God.

Amberley had never heard evolution taught as truth before. Mrs. Charin had mentioned it, but she had taught them that the Lord Jesus was God and that He had created all things. She had told them that some godless professors in the big universities believed in evolution, but that there was no proof it was true. Miss Collins was now teaching them that evolution was a fact—that they were not a special creation, but just an accident.

Miss Collins pulled down the roll-up map which hung over the chalkboard. On it was a beautifully colored chart, showing a great explosion of gases and how they had condensed into the stars, the planets, and our earth many billions of years ago. Teacher pointed to the various steps, showing how the solar system had evolved into what it is today.

"So you see, class, it has been proven beyond a doubt by science that evolution is a fact." Miss Collins smiled, smacking her wooden pointer against the chart. "And there will be a test next Friday on Chapter Eleven."

Amberley had always received good grades in science. She enjoyed hearing about the wonders of nature that only confirmed the greatness of God. Now everything she had been taught in church and by Mrs. Charin was being strongly challenged. Amberley did not want to admit it, but a seed of doubt seemed to be sprouting in her mind.

Eight
Amberley Tries To Cooperate Again

The remainder of the week was more of the same. Miss Collins taught them about the evolution of man and showed them another chart of strange-looking, hairy, ape-like men. She taught them that these weird creatures were their ancestors, and that after perhaps several million years, they had evolved into what man is today.

Miss Collins put the chart on the wall, and the students studied it during recess. The stoop-shouldered "men" had low, flat foreheads and bodies all covered in hair. Some of the boys laughed and made fun, but Amberley was not laughing. What if there was some truth to this? What if Pastor and Mrs. Charin were wrong? How would God fit into such a world?

As she stared at the chart, a sudden realization came over her mind.

If this is true, then the Bible cannot be true. If the scientists in the universities say that man evolved over millions of years and that everything was an accident, then what about my salvation?

Late that Friday evening after supper, Amberley sat next to Ma in her small but cheerful sewing room. The walls were painted pink, and the window was covered in fluffy lace curtains. It faced the big cornfield to the south. Ma's sewing machine was very old, and when it warmed up, it made the room smell like candle wax. Ma was repairing Dad's work shirts, and she seemed to sense that Amberley wanted to talk.

"What is it, dear?" she asked.

"Ma, I have tried very hard all week to be kind to Miss Collins, but—" Amberley drew silent.

"But what, dear?" Ma asked, snipping off some long threads.

"Oh Ma, am I really saved?"

"What!" Ma said. "Are you really saved? Where did you get such a notion?"

"Ma! Teacher showed us charts of ape-men and dinosaurs and exploding gases and told us about the millions and billions of years it took for them to evolve. My head was swimming," Amberley said, squeezing her head between her hands.

"Well," said Ma, "I wondered when this poison was going to invade our school."

Amberley looked puzzled. "What, Ma?"

Ma set down her sewing, took Amberley by both hands, and looked deep into her daughter's eyes. She spoke slowly and deliberately.

"Listen to me, sweetheart, and don't miss a word I'm going to say to you. There has been a battle going on for thousands of years; yes, ever since the week of creation and the beginning of time. Satan intensely hates God and His creatures. He hates everything that God has done, and ever since he lied to Eve in the Garden of Eden, man has become a fallen creature. Man is lost and needs a Savior. That is why the Lord Jesus had to come and die for us. He took our place to give fallen man a chance to come back to God and be saved. This makes Satan very angry. He tries to trick men into believing lies so they will not be saved. If man can be tricked into believing that everything evolved by accident, then he won't see himself as a sinner needing salvation. The Lord Jesus said of Satan, 'He is a liar, and the father of it.'"

Amberley bit her lip. "But Ma, these men in the big universities sound so smart."

"Dear, we are all a bit intimidated by people who have studied a lot and become our teachers. When I was in school, this same matter came up. We were confused even though we knew better. My best friend, even though she was a Christian, struggled with this problem all through school. Thank God I had a godly schoolteacher like your Mrs. Charin who kept us straight."

Ma spoke to her daughter firmly, putting her arm around her and pulling her close. "The Bible is the Word of God. God created the heavens and the earth, not billions of years ago, but more like six thousand years ago. God created man in His image, and we are very special to Him. Jesus is God and is the Creator. He is our dear Savior and died on the cross to take our place. Yes, Amberley, you are really saved." Ma squeezed Amberley hard as she finished.

"Ma, Teacher is going to give us a test next week on what she has taught us in science class. If I don't answer the questions as she has taught them, I'm going to fail. How can I write those answers down when I know they are lies and against the Bible?"

Ma frowned and shook her head. "It's such a tragedy that a young girl must be thrust into a grown-up battle so soon. Honey, you cannot betray the Word of God. You must first try to find a solution that will be pleasing to both God and man. Do you remember how we recently read about Daniel and how he dealt with a similar problem?"

Amberley nodded. "I remember in the Bible how Daniel was told that he must eat the king's food and drink his wine. He could have said 'No!' right off, but he tried to find a way to cooperate with Melzar, the prince of the eunuchs."

"That's right. Daniel was in training to become a leader, and the king thought that Daniel should eat the same food as a king. But the food was unhealthy and unlawful for a Jew to eat. Daniel made a deal with Melzar: if he would allow Daniel to eat vegetables and drink water for ten days, Daniel could prove that God's diet plan was best. After ten days, Melzar compared Daniel's complexion to the other young men who had eaten the king's food and drunk his wine. He was surprised when Daniel's face was brighter and healthier. Daniel was allowed to continue his diet of good vegetables and fresh water."

Ma smiled. "You see, honey, we must try to work out a solution, but if we cannot, we must always stand by the Word of God. Let's give the Lord a chance to work this out. Let's bow our heads and ask Him to remove the confusion and help you to know what to do."

Ma and Amberley knelt beside the stuffed chair in the little sewing room and asked the Lord for His guidance and wisdom. When they were through, Ma kissed Amberley's forehead and gave her a hug. The sweet fragrance of Ma's hair mixing with the hot wax smell of the antique sewing machine was good. It was the smell of home.

* * *

That Sunday, Ma and Amberley talked to Pastor Mitchell after the service about the evolution problem. He listened patiently, and when Amberley was finished, he fetched a book from his office.

"I want you to have this, Amber. It is a wonderful book about the creation and evolution issue. It was written by a great scientist who is a Christian. It is excellent and will explain the hoax of evolution. It has good solid answers for many of the things you have been taught in school."

"Thank you, Pastor," Amberley said, reaching out to take the book.

"The thing I want you to remember is that evolution is a religion and not a science. They cannot prove what they are telling you, because evolution is only a theory and cannot be observed or reproduced in a laboratory. The evolutionists must have more faith to believe in evolution than you do to believe in God."

Amberley spent the afternoon alone in her room, reading through the book that Pastor had given her. As she sat at her blue wicker desk by the window, the steam from her cup of hot cocoa made the pane fog up. She was surprised as she discovered just how flimsy the so-called evidence for evolution really was. Her spirits grew lighter and lighter as the truth of creation vindicated her faith in God and the Bible.

The following week, Amberley listened intently to Miss Collins's lectures on evolution. This time she took detailed notes and tried to create answers for them based on what she had read in Pastor's book.

"Class," Miss Collins said, pacing before the classroom, "you must understand that all life on earth evolved from a single-celled organism that became more and more complex. For example, fish evolved into amphibians—like frogs and salamanders. The amphibians evolved into reptiles such as lizards, the reptiles into birds and mammals, and finally, the mammals into man. This journey took millions of years and is backed up by the fossilized bones we find in the rock layers."

The story that Miss Collins was telling seemed so fanciful now that Amberley could only smile. The godly scientist who had written her book said there were no fossils in the ground or anywhere showing one type of animal evolving into another. A fish is always a fish, a frog a frog, and a man a man, just as God created them. Teacher had believed a lie and was now teaching that lie to her students.

Amberley intended to speak to Miss Collins before the test on Friday, but she wanted to be prepared for anything —regardless of the outcome.

Nine

Amberley Takes a Test and Is Tested

It was Friday morning, and Amberley decided to leave early for school. She arose from the breakfast table without a peep and took her coat and scarf off the hook behind the door.

"Amber, you have hardly touched your food," Ma commented, glancing at her husband.

"Amber, you need to finish your breakfast. Just because I'm working doesn't give us an excuse to waste food," Dad said sternly with a frown on his face.

But this was the day of the science test, and Amberley wanted to speak with Miss Collins before the rest of the students arrived. "Please, Daddy, I must get to school early today. I promise I will eat every bite on my plate if Ma will keep it for me until later. I must go."

Dad looked at the serious, desperate expression on his daughter's face and seemed to understand. "Very well," he said with a smile.

"Thank you, Daddy," she said, kissing him and Ma on the cheek. "Good-bye, Ma."

Amberley opened the door with a bang and held her breath, expecting the stinging cold to leap upon her like a wild animal. But instead, her face tingled with the warm, moist wind that had blown in during the night. She hurried to the schoolhouse, pleased that the streets were quite deserted. Rushing through the school entrance, she quickly hung up her coat in the cloakroom and brushed her hair in front of the little mirror over the water fountain. She paused before the door of the classroom, took several deep breaths, and pushed it open hard.

"Land sakes, girl!" Miss Collins exclaimed, holding her hand over her heart. "Are you trying to send me to the hospital? You are certainly early this morning."

Amberley took another deep breath and tried to calm her shaky voice. "Miss Collins, may I speak with you before the other students come in?"

She wanted to turn and run for the door. She quickly breathed a silent prayer: *Dear Lord, I'm so scared! Please help me, help me, help me!*

"Well, what is it, child? I'm very busy."

Amber swallowed. "Miss . . . Miss Collins? I know that you are a new teacher here and that this is only your first month at Sodus School. I also know that it hasn't been easy for you. I have tried to be a good student and not cause you any grief, but . . ."

Teacher began to fidget with the golden locket that hung from her neck.

"Spit it out, girl! But what?"

Miss Collins's thick-rimmed glasses seemed to grow larger and larger on her face. She had never looked so stern and menacing before. Amberley cleared her throat.

"I am a Christian," she said. "I believe that the Bible is the Word of God. Mrs. Charin was a Christian, too. She taught us that God created everything and that He created man in His own image. Now you are teaching us this evolution. If evolution is true, then the Bible cannot be true."

Amberley's mouth went dry, but she was gaining momentum, and her words spilled out of her. "Well, it is very confusing to us as students, and now you are going to give us a test today. If I put down what you have taught, then it will be the same as calling the Bible and Mrs. Charin liars."

Miss Collins looked very uneasy. She stood up, and her face grew as red as if it had been sunburned.

"Now you listen to me!" she snapped. "I am the teacher and you are the student! My responsibility is to teach you what I have learned at the university. I do not care to hear what your former teacher has taught you. What I am teaching you is the latest in scientific fact. If this does not agree with your personal beliefs, then I am sorry. There will be a test today on what you have been taught in science class. If your answers do not reflect what I have taught, they will be marked as wrong. If too many of them are marked wrong, you will fail. Is that understood? Now take your seat! Your fellow students are beginning to arrive!"

"Yes, ma'am," Amberley said as she drifted over to her seat. Her old desk by the window had always seemed like a friend. It was her place—but now it only felt like cold steel and wood. Miss Collins had spoken very unkindly to her, and she didn't seem to care at all about how she felt. She had tried to find a solution agreeable to both God and man, but Miss Collins had shot her down. She glanced back at the teacher, who had resumed her reading. There had been a ring of victory in her voice as she ordered Amberley to her desk. Amberley had never met anyone so cruel.

* * *

Amberley did not eat her lunch at noon, but sat still and watched the wind play in the snow outside the window. It was beginning to melt, and little drops of water could be seen dripping from the eves. She felt as if she was alone, and she didn't notice the low buzzing of conversation from the other students in the room. Perhaps she felt a bit like the Lord had let her down. Ma had told her many times that when you do something God's way, it will always turn out right in the end. But after speaking with Miss Collins, she didn't know what to think.

The bell rang, signaling the start of science class.

"Attention! Attention please! Class has begun. You will

remove everything from your desk except for a sharpened Number 2 pencil. I will pass out your science test, and you may begin as soon as you receive it."

Miss Collins quickly passed out the test papers to each student. She reminded Amberley of a robot. With the test paper on the desk before her, Amberley again gazed out of the window.

Dear Lord, Ma and Pastor Mitchell taught me to trust in You always, even when I don't understand. I have tried to do this Your way. I tried to speak with Miss Collins, but she will not hear me. Help me to answer these test questions so that I won't bring any shame on You or Your Word.

Amberley felt her eyes grow moist as she wrote her name at the top of the test paper. She read the first question:

1. WHAT IS THE APPROXIMATE AGE OF THE EARTH?

Amberley slowly wrote "6000 years" on the blank line. She knew that Miss Collins wanted her to put down "4.5 to 5 billion years" and that her answer would be marked wrong. She took a deep breath, and with a sigh, answered the rest of the questions. They were all the same: questions she could not answer the way Miss Collins wanted her to.

As she answered Question 9, "Who is considered the father of the science of evolution?" she remembered Pastor Mitchell's words about faith. "Charles Darwin," she wrote, "however, evolution is not a science but a belief requiring faith, just as I must have faith to believe in creation." The final question dared her to answer clearly, and she blinked back tears as she did it.

10. WHAT HAVE YOU LEARNED IN SCIENCE CLASS IN THE LAST TWO WEEKS WHICH HAS OPENED YOUR EYES TO THE TRUTH?

"My pastor says that there is no real truth aside from what is revealed in the Word of God. Anything that does not agree with the Bible is not truth. I do not mean to be disrespectful, but I cannot believe the teaching of evolution. The first verse in the Bible says that 'In the beginning God created the heaven and the earth.' If evolution is true, then my God and the Bible are liars."

Amberley put her pencil down and turned her test paper over. She felt miserable. Teacher soon collected all of the tests and graded them while the class studied. After recess, she handed the graded tests back. As Amberley had expected, she had failed. Teacher had given her one half point because she did answer "Charles Darwin" correctly.

Miss Collins dismissed school that afternoon and asked Amberley to remain behind. When the other students had left the room, Amberley approached the big wooden desk. Miss Collins finished some notes in her grade book and then, folding her hands, looked up at her student.

"Well, I see you have insisted on defying me after all. I told you what would happen if you did not answer the questions correctly."

"Yes, ma'am," Amberley said, "but I didn't want to

defy you. I just couldn't answer those questions in a way that I knew was against everything I believe in."

"Just the same, you have failed. If I were to give you a chance to take the test over, would it make any difference?"

"No, ma'am," Amberley said with a small smile, "it would not."

Miss Collins looked at Amberley for a moment, perhaps to see if her smile was meant in disrespect.

"I will say this, you are certainly not wanting in courage. You may go."

Amberley quickly put on her coat and scarf and gathered up her books. She burst out of the door into the steadily warming air. She knew that she had failed the science test, but she also felt the crushing weight lifted from her shoulders.

So this is what it is all about? she thought. *I tried to find a way to please my teacher without displeasing God. When that could not be done, I was left with only one choice, and that was to please God. I tried not to be disrespectful to Miss Collins, but I had to be true to God's Word. There was no other way for this to end. I am not happy that I failed, but I am happy that the Lord stood by me and helped me to do the right thing.*

When Amberley reached home, she had been so deep in thought that she barely remembered how she got there. Ma was getting dinner as usual when Amberley hung up her coat.

"Well, you are certainly a ray of sunshine." Ma smiled.

"Then everything went well today?"

"No, Ma," Amberley said as she sat at the kitchen table, breathing in the smell of roasting chicken and buttermilk biscuits.

Ma sat down next to her daughter. "Tell me all about it, sweetheart."

Amberley slowly reiterated the day's events. Ma reached over and brushed the hair from her daughter's serious eyes. "Well, I'm not happy that you failed, but I am pleased with the way you handled it. It took a lot of courage to stand up for the Bible. Most students would have put down the answers that the teacher wanted to see just to pass the test. God will not be ashamed of you, because you were not ashamed of Him."

Ten

Miss Collins Has Her Secret

All was cold and still in Sodus Township except for a few herds of deer browsing along the flooded ditches. It had rained continuously for three days and nights, melting all that was left of winter's snow. Early on the fourth night the skies finally cleared, and as the wispy scud clouds faded away like jets of steam, Orion and Pleiades twinkled brightly.

As the night moved on, the sleepy residents of Sodus were warm and secure in their beds. Contented before their cheerful fires, they were completely oblivious to a little Asian family that was trudging along the muddy shore of the St. Joseph River, desperately seeking a place to ford. Bewildered and exhausted, they frantically tried to find the road that would lead them back to Chicago.

"Daddy," the little girl said, "are we lost? Are we going to be back home soon?"

"No, my daughter, we are not lost," her father said bravely, taking off his old jacket and putting it across his daughter's shoulders. He indeed knew that they were lost, but he did not want to discourage his family any further. They were all so wet and tired, and he knew they could not go on much longer.

As he led his wife and daughter along the riverbank, he saw that it led into a thickly wooded hollow. The steadily thickening trees were familiar to him, reminding him of his jungle home in Vietnam. They moved ahead in the blackness until he ordered them to stop.

"This is a high place where we can build a shelter. It is near to the river, and we can fish and have a fire." He hoped his confident tone would encourage his frightened wife and daughter. He looked at his little girl with admiration; her clothing wet and muddy. She trusted him, and he could not let her down.

"Lien, you help me gather some sticks that are dry and will burn while your mother prepares us a supper."

Lien helped her father as her mother unwrapped the last of the dried fish she had kept secure in a bag of oilcloth. The ground was damp, and Lien began to shiver. Her black pajamas were suitable for a steamy jungle, but not for the Michigan woods in the springtime. Soon, her father had a fire burning, and the heat felt good. She stood with her back to it, pulling her father's coat about her tightly.

Her father worked to contrive a shelter by leaning dead branches against a tree and covering them with pine boughs. He layered pine boughs along the inside to make a bed and covered them with several old army blankets.

These had been a gift from a kindly American soldier he had befriended in Vietnam.

"Daughter, you climb into the shelter and cover up," Lien's mother ordered as she returned with a pot of water she had dipped from the nearby creek.

Lien watched her mother bring the water to a boil and throw in a handful of rice. As soon as the hard kernels began to bloom in the steamy pot, she put in the fish and took it off the smoky fire to rest.

"You come and eat now, Lien," she said, dishing out some rice and fish in a small bamboo bowl.

Lien was not really hungry, but her mother made her eat and drink some hot broth. It was good and helped to warm her, but all she wanted to do was sleep. Suddenly, a bright light flashed through the woods like a beacon.

"It's a helicopter! Get down!" her father shouted as he doused the fire, causing the pot of rice and fish to tumble down the hill. They had experienced many times the sudden deadly attacks of army helicopters in Vietnam and witnessed the destruction they could do. *How can this be happening here in America?* he thought.

Lien and her parents scurried under the makeshift shelter. As they lay low under the pine boughs, the bright beams of light flashed from one side of the hollow to the other. Finally, after ten minutes or so, the bright light went out, and a car motor could be heard driving away above the hill. Lien's heart was pounding as she lay frightened, huddled between her parents to keep warm.

* * *

Amberley helped Ma cut out a batch of biscuits for breakfast and put them in the hot oven while Dad read the paper at the table. As the biscuits swelled to a golden brown, Ma scrambled some eggs with just a little bit of grated cheese.

"Sam, my mother called this morning and told me that she had seen a light out in her woods last night. She called Officer Moore to investigate," Ma said as she poured Dad's cup of coffee.

"Well, that's curious. What did he find?"

"Apparently nothing. Moore drove up and down Hipps Hollow Road, shining his spotlight around, but he didn't see anything."

"It wouldn't be the first time she's had deer poachers in her woods. If she has any more trouble, I'll go out and take a look myself." Dad split a biscuit in half with his thumbs and stood, still cradling it in his hands. "But now I have to go to work."

* * *

The weeks went by, and as March arrived, a few warm, irresistible spring days began to appear. Pastor

Mitchell baptized Dad in the cool water of Pipestone Creek. Miss Collins was still very stern, but perhaps not as cold-hearted.

Maybe she is just warming up, like the weather, Amberley thought.

Miss Collins and Amberley had an unspoken understanding. Teacher seemed to secretly admire her student for her stand on evolution, and the compromising questions came less frequently in science class.

"Miss Collins?" Amberley said one morning, with more courage than she'd thought she had. "My mother baked you some banana bread. I hope you will like it." She handed Miss Collins the foil-wrapped loaf, still warm from the oven.

Miss Collins was grading papers at her desk and was visibly caught off guard. She pulled her thick-rimmed glasses down to the end of her nose and looked up at Amberley. "Why . . . why, thank you. That was very nice of you. Please thank your mother for me."

Amberley turned on her heels and returned to her desk. She tried to refrain from smiling lest Miss Collins misinterpret it.

* * *

The parent-teacher meetings were scheduled for late March, and Mary went in to meet Miss Collins. Amberley's grades were still very good in spite of her problems with science class. Mary had decided not to make an issue of what had happened. She would just be another conscientious mother concerned about her daughter's scholarship.

Mary entered the classroom at her appointed time. The room was empty except for Miss Collins. She stood to greet Mary and asked her to have a seat next to her desk. Mary sat down and watched Miss Collins intently as she opened her grade book to the name "Bridges."

Miss Collins turned to speak when Mary said, "Margaret?"

Miss Collins removed her heavy, thick-rimmed glasses in surprise and said, "Why, Mary—Mary Andrews?"

"Margaret Collins!" Mary said. "I haven't seen you since we went to high school together and you moved away. We were best friends and sang in the church choir and . . ." Mary stopped short and held her breath. The smile fled from her face.

"Oh, Margaret!" she said softly. "Can it be true? You are the Miss Collins who has been teaching this godless evolution to our children?"

A look of terrible self-contempt came over Miss Collins, and she appeared shaken. Now Mary was the stern one in charge as the teacher sat still to listen.

"Margaret! What has happened to you? You and I went forward in church and were saved the same night. We were baptized together. You were my best friend and one of the sweetest Christians I ever knew. Now you're teaching this satanic fairy tale to my daughter? What has happened to you?"

The heavy weight of shame and conviction could be seen on Margaret Collins's face as she wiped her eyes with a tissue. She paused. "Oh, Mary, I don't know what to say. How can I ever explain it to you?"

Mary was silent for several moments and then smiled.

She reached forward and patted Margaret's hand. "Come to dinner with us tonight."

"Mary, I couldn't . . . How could I face your daughter?"

"You let me worry about that. We live just up the road in the white house across from the coal yard." Mary wrote down her house number on a scrap of paper. "Anytime after five o'clock," she said, with a smile that still managed to be stern, "and don't let me have to come after you."

* * *

Ma said nothing to Amberley when she came home, but bustled about the kitchen getting supper.

"Come, dear," she said after a little while, "help me with dinner. Peel the potatoes and set them on to boil. Peel some apples, too. I'm going to make a pie."

Amberley waited for Ma to mention the parent-teacher meeting, but her mother said nothing about it. Amberley dug a handful of dusty potatoes out of the bin and sat at the table to peel them.

What did mean ol' Miss Collins say? she wondered.

Amberley closed her eyes tightly for a moment and pursed her lips. *I am sorry, dear Lord. I know better than to call her names.*

"I'm done with the potatoes and apples, Ma," she said, stuffing the peels into the garbage pail. "What else can I do?"

"Set an extra place for supper, Amber; we're having a guest."

"Who, Ma?"

"Just never you mind. You'll see soon enough."

Amberley set the extra place, wondering who her father might be bringing home for dinner. She thought nothing more of it until the clock struck five o'clock. A knock at the front door caused Ma to quickly set down a hot pie on the stove.

"Turn off the oven, Amber, while I get the door."

Amberley had been cleaning up after Ma, and her cheeks were dusty with flour. She was folding her apron when she heard a woman's voice talking with Ma in the living room.

"Amberley, come in here, please," Ma said.

Amberley closed the hot oven door and held the potholder in her hand as she obeyed. The "Yes, Ma" that began in the kitchen and trailed into the living room was cut short by the image of Miss Collins seated in Ma's chair. Amberley was in utter shock. The last person she had expected to see in her warm and secure world at that moment was Miss Collins. *Am I that bad of a student that Teacher must come to my house to speak with Ma?*

Miss Collins arose from the chair and timidly walked up to Amberley.

"Amberley, child, I know you may not be very happy to see me. I want to ask your forgiveness for the hard time I have given you this year."

Miss Collins offered her hand to Amberley. Her first sense was to recoil and run, but a quick glance from Ma made her stay.

Reaching forward with caution, Amberley met Miss Collins's hand and held it. It was warm, and Miss Collins's smile disarmed her.

"I know that this may be hard for you to believe, but your mother and I grew up together and were best friends. I hope that you and I might become friends, also," Teacher said sincerely.

A bang from the kitchen door announced that Dad was home. He walked into the living room and found everyone in tears.

"What's all this?" he said.

Ma wiped her tears and said, "Sam, this is Margaret Collins, Amberley's new schoolteacher, come to have supper with us."

Dad looked surprised. "Hello, Miss Collins. Are you the new teacher who started just after Christmas vacation?"

"No," Ma laughed, "this is a brand new teacher who just started today!"

* * *

School took on a different flavor when the students found out that Miss Collins could be as sweet as Mrs. Charin. She began her first day back in class by telling Herbie Johnson to "Smile and keep on smiling. That's an order!" Science class was no longer so cold and dreadful either. Miss Collins endeavored to teach both creation and evolution, explaining that both were beliefs that required a great deal of faith from their believers.

Miss Collins and Amberley became good friends. The teacher eventually joined their church, and Amberley found out how pleasant her voice could be when she sang in the choir with Ma. She still did not understand Miss Collins's story and the reason for her transformation. Ma told her that Miss Collins would explain everything to her in her own good time.

Then one Friday, Miss Collins asked Amberley to see her after school. As she approached her desk, she could see that Miss Collins was sober and not smiling.

"What is it, Miss Collins?" she asked, sensing that

something was different. "Did I do something wrong?"

"Sit down, child," Miss Collins said, nodding her head at the chair beside her desk. "I have something to tell you."

Amberley held her breath, knowing that nothing good ever followed a sentence like that.

"Today is my last day at Sodus School. I have an opportunity that just came up, and if I take it, I must leave right away."

Amberley felt tears begin to flow down her cheeks. She slowly stood up and went to Miss Collins, putting her arms around her.

"But Miss Collins . . ."

"Tut, child, none of that. Please don't say anything more. This is hard for me too."

"But will I ever see you again? Will you write me a letter sometime and tell me how you are doing?"

"I will write you, and I promise you that if it is possible, I will see you again. Perhaps you will be a fine young lady then, and I can have you over for tea. Now, no more of this," she said, wiping away Amberley's tears with her thumb. "You must go home now, or I will never be able to leave."

"Yes, ma'am," Amberley said, turning slowly to walk out the door.

"Wait a moment, dear," Miss Collins said. "Come here."

Amberley turned slowly and walked back to Miss

Collins's desk.

Miss Collins reached up and slid the thick-rimmed glasses off her face, folded them, and handed them to Amberley.

"Here—a keepsake for you. I know you kids laughed at them, and I don't blame you." She chuckled. "I've decided to try contact lenses."

"Thank you, Miss Collins. I will keep them always."

Eleven

The Problem With Brenda

The spring weather was unusually warm, and after breakfast, Amberley started out for school without putting on her jacket. Ma stopped her at the door.

"Amber, don't let this nice weather deceive you. Put on your jacket. It could turn cold and rainy in a moment's time," Ma exhorted her. "Do you want to get sick and miss out on this weekend?"

"No, Ma," Amberley said, zipping up her blue jacket. She skipped down the back steps and stopped to inspect Ma's purple crocuses. They were beautiful against the yellow spirea bushes that bordered the backyard. She was indeed excited about the coming weekend, because Dad was taking them to Grandma Andrews's farm. They loved Grandma's place along Hipps Hollow and the St. Joseph River. This was the farm where Ma had been born and spent her childhood. Hipps Hollow was only a few miles away, but it always felt like another world, with its vast open fields on one side and the great hollow that opened up to the flats along the river.

Amberley was especially looking forward to this trip because Dad wanted to come along too. He had always avoided doing family things with them, staying home where he could be free to drink. Now he seemed to relish the thought of spending the weekend with them.

Amberley so wanted to get to know her father better. All of those years before his conversion were spent in a seemingly endless cycle of drinking and then apologizing when he became sober. Now Dad had thrown himself into Bible study and church activities. He was trying so hard to be the father that Amberley had always wished she'd had.

Amberley's new teacher was Miss Sullivan. This was her first year teaching, and everyone seemed to like her. She was so young and spirited that Amberley almost forgot she was the teacher.

Miss Sullivan had taken an interest in Amberley, and they became friends. She took time to teach her student some French during the long lunch hour and encouraged her to try writing. At recess, though, Amberley liked to be by herself on the big swing at the edge of the schoolyard. This corner overlooked a large valley-like expanse of field with a view that she found beautiful and soothing. There were acres of manicured grape vines, tart cherry orchards, and blueberries in the wet lowlands where nothing else would grow. She would get so caught up in thought that once she didn't hear the bell and walked into class fifteen minutes late. The other students giggled, but Miss Sullivan didn't scold her because Teacher was a bit of a dreamer too.

When Amberley arrived at school that morning, she noticed a new girl standing alone by the bookcase at the back of the room. She was very tall for her age and had long jet-black hair parted down the middle. When the bell rang, she took the desk in the corner at the end of Amberley's row. *Perhaps she might become my new best friend,* she thought.

"Class," Miss Sullivan said, "I want to introduce a new student, Brenda Bickel. Please stand up, Brenda."

Brenda kept her seat and didn't look up. She pretended not to hear Miss Sullivan.

"Brenda? Would you like to say hello to the class?" Miss Sullivan said, her tone still gentle. Brenda looked at Teacher and frowned. The room hushed, and Amberley gasped. She had never seen anyone openly defy a teacher before.

Miss Sullivan cleared her throat. "Well, then, class. Let's get out our books for English."

If Miss Sullivan allows this to pass, it will only encourage others to do the same thing, Amberley thought. But Miss Sullivan said nothing.

Amberley observed Brenda the rest of that day. She didn't seem to be a very happy girl, and she usually walked around by herself. She had a perpetual scowl on her face and acted tough when the other girls came near.

The next day at recess, Amberley quickly walked

across the schoolyard to her usual place on the end swing. The fifteen-minute recesses always flew by when she was swinging, but she couldn't help herself. This particular day, she had no sooner sat down when she heard a gruff voice from behind.

"Hey, Red, that's my seat!"

Amberley turned around. Brenda Bickel stood behind her with several of the other girls.

"Hey, Red, are you deaf? I said that's my seat. Now move!"

With that, Brenda grabbed the chain and pushed Amberley off the swing. She landed with such a great thud that her teeth clicked together as she hit the ground. She looked up to see Brenda sitting in her swing and the other girls laughing and snickering at her embarrassment. Some of the girls were her friends.

The ringing of the recess bell ended the ordeal as Brenda and the girls left Amberley alone to return to class. Amberley rose painfully to her feet and dusted off her dress, attempting to control her bewilderment. She had been humiliated by a bully and hurt by her friends. A bully she could understand, but how could those other girls be so cruel to her?

She watched Judy Bailey and Joan and Becky Hartman crowd around Brenda like puppy dogs. These girls had grown up with her. She had spent the night at their homes and eaten at their tables.

Later that night she told Ma the story. She was embarrassed to share this particular problem, but Ma always gave such good advice.

Ma smiled. "I'm not laughing at you, dear. It's just that all the things that are happening to you have happened to me, too, at one time or another. School wouldn't be school if there wasn't at least one bully."

Ma sat at the table next to her daughter. "You are so very serious about everything, Amber, and these things surprise you as they come along. But you are traveling a road of life that many girls have walked before."

Amberley wasn't any too comforted by this answer, and she grimaced in reply.

"But Ma, why must there be bullies? Why does Brenda Bickel hate me? I haven't done anything to her."

Ma wiped her hands on her apron and picked up her big Bible from the table. She read I Corinthians 10:13: "There hath no temptation taken you but such as is common to man: but God is faithful, who will not suffer you to be tempted above that ye are able; but will with the temptation also make a way to escape, that ye may be able to bear it."

Ma explained, pointing to the word with her finger, "The word 'temptation' in this verse also means testing or trial. The problem you are having with this new girl is not a new thing, dear. It is 'common to man.' According to this verse, you have God's promise that as a Christian, you will be able to handle any trial that comes along."

"Does that include bullies like Brenda Bickel?" Amberley asked.

"Even bullies," Ma said.

* * *

As Amberley was leaving for school the next morning, she picked up her books and her sack lunch from the table. She kissed Ma on the cheek and turned to open the door.

Ma was doing the breakfast dishes, but she turned away from the suds to speak to Amberley before she left. "Honey, I know that I throw a lot of Bible verses at you sometimes, but I want you to learn to handle your problems God's way. So many Christians fail during times of trial and testing. No matter what happens to you in life, there is a Bible promise or principle to guide you. Sometimes God's Word will give you a direct command, like 'Thou shalt not.' Other times it will give you principles and guidelines to follow that are more flexible. God's Word always has the right answer."

Amberley listened intently to her mother with her hand still on the doorknob, knowing from past experience that Ma was usually right.

"The problem with Brenda is that something is broken inside. We don't know anything about her home or parents. Try to be as kind and understanding as you can."

"Thanks, Ma. I'll try," Amberley said as she bid her mother good-bye.

Amberley was early on her way to school, so she stopped at the little park called the Point in the center of town, where Pipestone and Naomi Roads came together and framed the park like a slice of pie. She sat on the wooden bench and asked God to help her deal with Brenda. She had learned from the experience with Miss Collins that it was easier to be nice to someone when she had first invested prayer in them.

* * *

School that day was so far uneventful, as Brenda was busy with her newfound gang of friends. Miss Sullivan had given the class time to study before recess. The room was quiet, and Amberley was engrossed in her book. Suddenly, she felt the girl behind her tap her shoulder. She turned out of reflex as the girl handed her a folded note. She took the note without thinking—and then she heard Miss Sullivan's voice.

"Amberley? Are you passing notes in class?"

"No . . . no, ma'am!" Amberley stammered.

Teacher's voice made her surprise obvious. "Please bring that note up here to me."

Amberley was horrified at what was happening to her. She had always been the good girl who sat quietly while the others misbehaved. Now she had been caught passing notes in class.

Slowly, Amberley stood up and glanced behind her. Some of the other girls were giggling and holding their hands over their mouths. Brenda Bickel was smiling a sinister smile, and Amberley heard her say under her breath, "How do you like that, Teacher's Pet?"

"Please read the note out loud for everyone to hear, Miss Bridges," Teacher ordered. Amberley had never been addressed as "Miss Bridges" before. She felt sick. Could this be happening to her? She slowly unfolded the note and read the words to herself. She turned to Teacher's desk and mournfully said, "Oh Miss Sullivan, I can't read this out loud."

"Please read the note as I have asked you to do," Miss Sullivan said sternly.

Amberley cleared her throat and read what Brenda had written on the paper:

> Miss Sullivan has pretty eyes of blue,
> Her brain's as sharp as a tack.
> But she sounds so stupid speaking French,
> In her dress made of gunnysack!

The class roared with laughter. Amberley felt helpless as she turned to look at Teacher. Miss Sullivan just sat behind her desk, looking so small. Amberley felt like a traitor. Miss Sullivan had been so kind to her, teaching her French and encouraging her to write. Amberley could see the hurt in Teacher's face. She wanted to run far away and never come back to Sodus School again.

Mercifully, the recess bell rang, and Miss Sullivan halfheartedly dismissed the class. Amberley remained behind. When they were all alone, she went to Miss Sullivan's desk and stood silently. Miss Sullivan folded a few papers and coldly ignored her.

"Please, Miss Sullivan, you must let me explain."

Teacher spoke without looking up. "Hadn't you better go to recess with your friends?"

"Oh, Miss Sullivan!" Amberley cried out. "Miss Sullivan!"

Miss Sullivan stacked her papers hard on the desk. "I suppose this is what is meant by not casting your pearls before swine!" she said with great emotion.

"Please, Miss Sullivan, I didn't write this note. It was handed to me and I just took it. Look at the handwriting. It's not mine."

Amberley spread the note on the desk in front of Miss Sullivan. The desk and Teacher were little more than a blur through Amberley's tears.

"See, this is not my handwriting."

Miss Sullivan read the note without touching it.

"You didn't write this?"

"No, ma'am. I would never, ever do anything like this

83

to you or any other teacher. You have been so kind to me. You have been my friend. I could never do this to you."

Miss Sullivan stared at the note for a moment and then chuckled to herself, her eyes still glassy. "I didn't want to believe that you would do something like this, Amber," she said, wiping a tear from her eye. She stood up and smiled at Amberley. "I'm glad it wasn't you."

She gave Amberley a quick hug. "Now hush! Go to recess, and we'll talk about it later."

"Yes, ma'am," Amberley said, and she went out to wash her face.

Twelve

The True Friend

Miss Sullivan did talk to Amberley after school about Brenda Bickel. She had known a few bullies in her day, but dealing with them as a teacher was a new experience for her. They hoped that Brenda would soon weary of her games and the other girls would lose interest.

"I think that bullies get their courage from the crowd that supposes they are big shots. They sort of feed off of each other," Teacher said. "Anyway, there is more going on with Miss Brenda than meets the eye."

After the supper dishes were washed that evening, Amberley did her homework in her room. Dad was busy studying a Bible course that Pastor Mitchell had given him. It was strange to see him anywhere near a Bible after all these years. He had yielded his life to the Lord, and the changes in him were remarkable.

Amberley had been so absorbed in handling Brenda Bickel that she had almost forgotten about their coming weekend at Grandma's farm. She had seen Jimmy Hansen riding by on his buckskin horse, and the animal reminded her of Gray, Grandma Andrews's good and faithful horse. But tomorrow was only Wednesday, and she didn't know if she could last the whole week. What would Brenda do to her next? Would the weekend ever come? Amberley sighed and finished her homework and an assignment in French that Miss Sullivan had given her.

It was a warm, pleasant evening. The sky was blue except for the reddish-orange clouds westward over Lake Michigan. Ma was seated at the kitchen table, looking through a seed catalog, and Dad sat next to her, reading his paper over a cup of coffee.

"May I go for a short walk, Ma?" Amberley asked, walking into the kitchen.

"If it's all right with your father."

"Dad, I . . ."

"Just don't go too far, and be back before the sun sets."

"Yes, sir," said Amberley as she slipped on her jacket hanging by the back door. Amberley's feet crunched on the gravel in the alleyway. She saw no one outside, nor any traffic on the street. She was alone except for God.

Dear Lord Jesus, please protect me as I walk and talk with You. Show me how to deal with Brenda Bickel. Ma says that she has something broken inside. Please help me make friends with her before she breaks something inside of me.

Amberley walked down the quiet street to the deserted schoolyard. It would be nice to swing for a while and clear her thoughts. At least she wouldn't get beaten up

86

when she finished. But as she rounded the empty schoolhouse, she stopped and caught her breath. Someone was sitting in one of the swings. Amberley quickly turned to leave, but something stopped her.

The person sitting in the swings looked like Brenda Bickel.

Amberley's first impulse was to run all the way home. *It would be bad enough to get beat up during school hours with dozens of witnesses looking on,* she thought. *It would be really stupid getting beat up after school all alone.*

She wanted to sneak away, but her feet wouldn't move. All she could do was stand and stare at Brenda. Then Amberley felt a shock of surprise. Brenda appeared to be crying, and she was holding her arm as if in pain. Amberley suddenly felt a surge of compassion. Here was this smug, self-confident bully who needed no one but herself, revealing in secret that she was very human indeed.

As Amberley walked toward Brenda, she noted how helpless and frail the taller girl looked.

I may get beat up, she thought, *but I need to see if she's all right.*

"Brenda?" she said softly. "Are you okay?"

Brenda's eyes showed that she was startled. "What do you want?" she growled.

"Are you hurt? Is your arm all right?"

Brenda stood up, letting the swing sway behind her. "Get out of here and leave me alone!"

"Brenda, all I want to do is help you," Amberley said, pointing to Brenda's injured arm.

"Well, I don't need a goody-goody to help me, so get lost!"

The sun was even lower in the sky now, casting shadows across the playground and making it harder to see the tears on Brenda's face. But Amberley knew they were there—she could hear them in Brenda's voice. "Brenda, I just want to be your friend."

The words seemed to melt Brenda's hard shell a bit, and she began to weep again.

"Why would you or anyone else want to be my friend? I am a worthless waste of air space. Anyway, that's what my old man keeps telling me."

Amberley was shocked by Brenda's bitter words. She moved next to the bully and put her hand on her shoulder.

"How can you say that? No one is worthless—especially you."

Brenda sniffed. "I am worthless because nobody loves me or wants me. My old man told me so. He said I was a mistake, and the only reason he keeps me around is for the welfare money. He said my mother begged him and made him promise to take care of me before she died. If it wasn't for that, he would have put me in a foster home long ago."

Amberley could scarcely believe what she was hearing. Ma was right. Brenda did have something broken inside. She thought about Dad and how hard he worked to

88

provide, and about Ma who was always there for her with godly counsel. She remembered her Savior's loving arms that held her as she drifted off to sleep. What must it be like to honestly believe that no one really loved you or wanted you?

Amberley summoned all of her courage and said, "Brenda, I know two people who love you very much."

The words sounded strange and dull to Amberley's ears, and she couldn't tell for a moment if she had really spoken them.

Brenda was quiet now, and she sat back down in the swing.

"Who could love me?" she asked.

"I do, for one, and the Lord Jesus. That's two people who love you, and you said that no one did. I love you because I am a Christian. The Lord Jesus loves you because He died for you."

Brenda looked up at Amberley and said, "That's what my old man calls religious bunk. I know you hate me for the way I treated you, and if Jesus loved me, he wouldn't have killed my mother and given me a drunken old man who hates me and beats me!"

Brenda's hurt and anger almost took Amberley's breath away. *She has never known what it is like to have a sweet home life,* Amberley thought. *She is nothing but a way for her father to get drinking money.*

Amberley put her arm around Brenda. "Brenda, have

you had anything to eat? Won't you come home with me and let my mother make you something? It's getting dark and chilly."

Amberley was surprised when Brenda nodded.

"Will your father mind that you are out?" Amberley asked.

Brenda gave a half-smile. "He doesn't even know I'm alive."

When they reached the white house, Amberley told her parents all about Brenda's situation. Ma held Brenda in her arms, and the former bully seemed to dissolve in response to her love and kindness. She wept a good while until she could do nothing else but sleep.

* * *

Later, Sam and Mary went into the kitchen to discuss Brenda. Sam was disgusted and did not try to hide his anger.

"If I did what I felt like doing right now, I would probably be arrested. How could a man beat up his own daughter, even if he was drunk? I think I'm going to pay Bickel a little visit!"

"No, Sam," Mary said. "I know you are upset, and so am I. No wonder this child is like she is—but you ending up in jail will not help Brenda. Please promise me you won't go."

Sam smiled an assuring smile. "Don't worry, Mary; I'm not going to do anything rash. Maybe I should just call the police."

"Sam, she made me promise that I wouldn't. Bickel is her father, and she has regard for him in spite of the kind of man he is. Maybe Pastor Mitchell could help."

Sam called Pastor Mitchell, and the two of them went to visit Mr. Bickel. They drove down a long narrow dirt road that led to some abandoned migrant cabins. They stopped in front of the only one that could possibly be inhabited, for it had smoke coming out of the chimney and most of the windows were intact. Evidently, the farmer had allowed Brenda and her father to stay there in exchange for doing some odd jobs around the farm.

Sam and Pastor were appalled at what they saw. There were several rusted metal drums filled with trash by the door. Their contents consisted mostly of old wine and whiskey bottles. The wooden steps to the cabin were broken, and the walls were stained green with moss.

As Sam and Pastor walked up to the front door, they noticed that it was ajar. Sam peered into the darkness of the cabin as the stench clutched his throat. He felt along the wall for a light switch until he heard it click. A solitary bulb hanging from the openly raftered ceiling revealed an unconscious man laying in his own vomit. Sam kneeled down and checked the man's breathing and pulse.

"He is very weak," Sam said. "He's not sleeping, but

he's drunk himself into a stupor."

"Are you sure, Sam?" Pastor asked.

"I was cross-trained as a medical specialist in the Special Forces. Besides," Sam paused, "I know drunk when I see it. He needs to get to a hospital soon or he might die."

* * *

The next morning, Brenda opened her eyes and stared at the ceiling. She quickly sat up. *Where am I?* she thought. Nothing looked familiar.

"Good morning, honey," a sweet, red-haired lady said, as she walked into the front room. *Amberley's mother.* "Did you sleep well?"

Brenda rubbed her eyes as she sat up, letting the blanket fall away from her temporary bed on the couch. "Yes, ma'am."

"Good," Amberley's ma said. "Amberley will be down shortly, and you can have breakfast. Do you like pancakes?"

"Yes, ma'am," Brenda said again, still trying to remember the events of last night.

Amberley's ma sat down next to Brenda on the couch. "Sweetie, before Amberley comes down, I want to talk to you. Your father is in the hospital and very sick. We will take you to see him when you are ready."

Fear jumped up in Brenda's throat. "Is . . . is he going to die?" she asked, putting her hand on the side of her face.

"I think he will be all right, Brenda. He just needs to get well, and that may take a long time."

"Where am I to stay, ma'am? I don't have any family." Fear and agitation gripped Brenda, and she tried to swallow them back. Amberley's mother scooted closer to Brenda, putting her arm around her. "You are staying with us, dear. Our pastor fixed it with the court to let you stay with us until your father is well. Is that okay with you?"

"Yes, ma'am, I would like that," Brenda said. The panic in her heart seemed to subside a little.

"Then it's settled," Amberley's ma said, planting a kiss on Brenda's forehead. "And after breakfast, you and Amberley can go down the alley to Mrs. Enkins's house. She has a bed for you, and we'll set it up in Amberley's room."

A sudden clatter announced Amberley's arrival as she hurried down the stairs. "Ma, I overslept. I don't have enough time to get ready for school."

"You and Brenda are staying home from school today. I want to get her settled in. She needs some new clothes and some other things."

Amberley sat next to her mother on the couch as Brenda moved over to make room for her. "What, Ma?"

"Brenda is going to live here with us as long as she likes," her mother said, holding Brenda close. "And we want her to stay, too, don't we Amber?"

Amberley squealed. "Oh, Brenda, won't that be fun?

I've never had a sister before!"

Brenda only smiled. She didn't know what to think.

Thirteen
Sometimes It Takes a Bully

As the days swiftly passed, Brenda became more and more accustomed to her new surroundings. She was a bit timid at first, but she responded well to the genuine love that radiated like sunshine from her new home—love like she had never known before.

Brenda happily shared the endless responsibilities of home life. It turned out that she knew a lot about cooking. Amberley had asked Ma's permission to make supper one evening. It was nearing time for Dad to come home from work, and Ma stepped into the kitchen to check on her progress. She was met with the delicious aroma of a roast.

"What is that wonderful smell?" Ma said, sniffing the air.

"It's roast pork, Ma, with carrots and onions and potatoes," Amberley said with a beaming smile.

"But how . . . I thought you were just going to make grilled cheese sandwiches? And is that bay leaf?" Ma said, clearly surprised.

"It was Brenda, Ma. She showed me how to do it." Amberley put her hand on Brenda's shoulder.

Brenda blushed. "Amber, it wasn't a big deal."

"Child, where did you learn to cook like that?" Ma asked with a smile.

"Oh, I don't really know how to cook." Brenda blushed again. "It's just that when my pa was—well, you know—I would spend hours at the library reading mostly cookbooks. I haven't done much cooking. Most of what I know is what I have read."

Brenda reached down and picked up an old, worn-out book from the edge of the table. The cover had been repaired many times, and several pages hung loose. She held it up proudly for Ma to see. "This is my mother's old cookbook. I asked your husband if he would go and get if for me. It's all I have that belonged to her." Ma took the book from Brenda's hands and thumbed through it delicately.

"Some of Pa's friends that knew my ma said she was beautiful, kind, and a wonderful cook; at least that's what they say. I wanted so much to be like her. That's why I studied cooking and nearly inhaled every cookbook I could get my hands on."

"If your ma could see you now, she would be so pleased with you. And I appreciate you taking Amberley under your wing," Ma said, giving Brenda a hug.

"Thank you, Brenda," Amberley said, putting her

oven mitts on. "Before you came, all I could do was cut out a few biscuits."

* * *

The girls walked the short morning walk to Sodus School. They could smell the sugary apple cider that seemed to fill every molecule of the air. The presses at the fruit exchange were pressing the last of the cold storage apples into juice, and a fragrant steam hung in the cool spring air like a cloud above Sodus.

It was Friday, and Amberley had to contain her excitement. Dad was finally taking them to the farm for the weekend. Brenda would be meeting Grandma Andrews for the first time.

In the classroom, Brenda shyly presented a loaf of banana bread she had baked the night before to Miss Sullivan. The teacher thanked her very much and smiled to herself over Brenda's transformation.

"Thank you, dear," Teacher said. "It is so good to see you smile."

* * *

At afternoon recess, Amberley and Brenda headed for the swings where they had first met. Brenda excused herself to speak with Miss Sullivan, so Amberley went on ahead. As she walked across the big schoolyard, she was surprised to see a crowd of students gathered around the swings. She could hear loud voices and shouting as the crowd shuffled back and forth. As she came nearer, she saw that it was a fight.

"Fight" was perhaps not the best word, for only one boy was doing the hitting. The new boy, Joe Schenkle, was pushing around another new boy who had just moved to Sodus and lived down the alley from Amberley. He was much younger and smaller than Joe, and his name was Billy Gussette.

Billy was frantically trying to escape from Joe, but to no avail. The bully would just catch him and trip him up each time he ran away. He looked so pathetic with his dirty, grass-stained face and bleeding, runny nose.

Amberley was filled with disgust! Little Billy was being beaten to a pulp, and no one seemed willing to help. She ran through the crowd without thinking and pushed Joe from behind. He hardly moved. The big, strong farm boy, obviously accustomed to having his way, turned and struck Amberley across the face!

She heard nothing as she hit the ground with a thud. Her whole body seemed to go numb, and her vision was filled with swirling splashes of color and light. But all at once her hearing returned, and the searing pain in her face hit like an explosion! She tried to pick herself up off of the ground, but she quickly sought to rest her face against the cool grass to soothe the pain.

"Anybody else want summa this?" Joe boasted, waving his big dirty fist in the air. "I hits girls or boys— don't matter none to me!"

The terror of Joe Schenkle settled on the crowd of students like a soft hush. They looked at him, not knowing whether to smile or keep their faces expressionless. They collectively stood frozen, afraid to speak, move, breathe, or do anything which might be interpreted as a challenge, hoping that the warm spring sunshine would melt them into the schoolyard without so much as a peep.

Amberley sat on the ground next to Billy, two kindred victims of a giant named Joe Schenkle. No student dared to help them or to even see to their wounds. The whole ordeal seemed to last for half an hour, though in reality it was but a few moments.

Amberley glanced up at Joe with his red face and slicked-back hair. She could hear Billy softly crying beside her. Dad had once mentioned the Schenkle boys who lived in Shanghai, a cluster of houses in Pipestone Township. He had gone to school with Joe's father and uncles.

"Just a gang of punks and hoodlums!" he had commented with disgust. The memory of Dad's voice made Amberley feel stronger and filled her with resolve. Dad and Ma did not approve of fighting, but they did tell her that she had the right to defend herself or someone else.

"When the Bible says to turn the other cheek, it doesn't

mean to stand there and let someone beat you up," Dad had once said. With the memory, Amberley felt her head clear and her strength returning.

Somebody has to stop that bully, or none of us will be able to leave the school building except to run home in fear!

Amberley stood up on rubbery legs to face Joe again and let him know that she wasn't afraid. Of course, she *was* afraid—but more than that, she was indignant.

Joe grinned. He reminded Amberley of a smiling ape. He raised his hard, dirty fist high, like an Olympic torch for all to see. He walked swiftly toward her, and she closed her eyes hard in anticipation of what was to come.

Smack! The sound was loud and crisp. Amberley waited for pain to blister through her face, but it never came. A loud cheer from the crowd made her peek out of the one eye that would open. There, lying on his back, dazed and groaning, was Joe Schenkle. Goliath had been slain—but by whom?

Amberley turned around, and there, standing tall and terrible, was Brenda. Her beautiful black hair shone like raven's feathers in the afternoon sun.

"Whut happened? Who hit me?" Joe moaned, rubbing his face with his formerly mighty hand.

Brenda walked over to Joe and reached down to clutch his shirt. Buttons flew in all directions. She yanked him into a sitting position.

"I hit you!" she growled. "My name is Brenda Bridges,

and the girl you hit is my little sister. If I ever see or hear of you touching her again, you won't be much good to your pa for chores, I can promise you that!"

Brenda released his shirt, and Joe fell back on the grass with a thud. A cheer rang out across the schoolyard, only to be quickly hushed as the figure of Miss Sullivan hurried toward them.

"Children, children, what is going on here?" she called.

Jackie Taylor, one of the Taylor twins, quickly spoke up.

"Miss Sullivan, we were just playing a game, and I guess it got out of hand." She smiled sheepishly as Miss Sullivan studied her face.

"A game? Are you sure?"

"Yes, ma'am." All of the students seemed to chime in at once.

"It was only in fun," Vickie Taylor said.

Miss Sullivan looked at Billy Gussette and Amberley with all of their dirt and scratches, not sure of what to say or think. Then the moans from the grass behind the crowd told her the whole story. A teacher friend of hers from Shanghai School had warned her about Joe. She knew that Joe Schenkle was a ruffian, but she didn't know what to do about him. She turned to look at Brenda, who was standing with her eyes bright and her fists clenched, deliberately avoiding Miss Sullivan's eyes.

"Brenda, you are mighty quiet," Teacher said.

Brenda looked up at Miss Sullivan. "Yes, ma'am."

Teacher fought to hide a smile. "Well, children, no more playing games today!" she said sternly.

Miss Sullivan turned and made her way back to the school building with a slight skip in her step. She was elated that Joe had suffered a little street justice, but she couldn't let the students know how she felt.

Brenda helped Amberley and Billy back to the schoolhouse to tend to their wounds.

"I'm glad you didn't forget how to fight," Amberley said as they made their way across the schoolyard.

"Just remember, Amber, sometimes it takes a bully to handle a bully." Brenda smiled.

Young Billy looked up at Brenda with awed adoration. Little heart-shaped bubbles could almost be seen floating around his face.

"Wow, Brenna! You sure can fight good!" he gushed.

The girls looked at each other and chuckled as they glanced back at the figure of Joe, seated on the ground with his head buzzing like a beehive.

Brenda put her hand on Billy's shoulder and said, "Let's go, kid."

Fourteen

Sam Renders His Verdict

The girls walked the half-mile home with Billy Gussette tagging behind. They took him to his door and explained to his mother what had happened.

She could hardly contain her gratitude. "We really don't know a lot of people here yet, and it makes me feel good that someone is looking after Billy. I'm a widow, you know, and he is all I have."

The girls walked to the tiny wedged-shaped park in the center of town to discuss what they should tell their parents about the fight. Dad and Ma would not be happy about it, and Amberley would not be able to hide her black eye.

"I say that we tell them nothing about the fight. As far as your folks are concerned, you got hit in the face by a softball," Brenda said, making a throwing gesture.

Amberley looked at the ground and bit her lip.

"What is it?" Brenda asked, noting that Amberley was squirming.

"Brenda, I couldn't lie to my parents. I would rather

103

take my medicine than try to deceive them. Besides, it would be like lying to God too." Then Amberley said, with a timid smile, "Yeah, I know. I'm just a 'goody-goody.'"

"Yes, you are." Brenda grinned, turning Amberley by her shoulders toward home. "Let's go take our medicine."

Dad moved the discussion about the fight to after dinner. With the dishes washed and put away, he presided in his big chair like Solomon on his throne. He listened intently to their narratives and then waited in silence to pass judgment.

When they were finished, he said thoughtfully, "I don't see how it could have gone any other way. I've known a few bullies in my day, and a bloody nose, sometimes, is all they will understand. I am very happy with you, Amber, for going to the rescue of that little boy, and with you, Brenda, for coming to the defense of Amberley. I also think you have a very wise and discerning teacher. The matter is closed as far as I am concerned."

As Dad spoke the last part of the sentence, he interlocked his fingers and looked away as if he truly were a judge making ready for his next case. The girls gave him a hug and kiss and said, "Thank you, Daddy."

Ma began to chuckle to herself and then put her hand over her mouth as if to change the subject.

"What is it, Mary?" Dad asked.

"I was just remembering when I was about the girls' age and an older girl would chase me home from school every day."

"What a bully!" Amberley said.

"Yes, and she beat up a lot of girls in my school. I knew if she ever caught me, it was going to be Saturday night in Sioux City." Amberley smiled at Ma's favorite phrase, a line from an old cowboy movie, as her mother continued. "I was pretty fast, and I always made it to the mailbox at Grandpa Andrews's long driveway just in time."

"Oh, Ma, what did you do?" asked Brenda.

"Well, this went on for several weeks until the first snowfall. That particular day, I shot out of the schoolhouse door, and the girl was fast on my heels as usual. As we rounded the corner by our farm, she caught me. She grabbed the back of my long hair, and we both fell and tumbled along the icy gravel road. As luck would have it, though, I landed on top of her, and without missing a stroke, I thrashed the daylights out of her with all my might. She never bothered me again after that, and as I recall, we became pretty good friends."

"That was a good story, Ma," Amberley said, laughing and exchanging glances with Brenda.

"You see, girls, a Christian shouldn't go about picking fights or being a bully, but we all have the right to defend ourselves. Now, off to bed. Morning comes early, and your dad wants to get an early start to Grandma Andrews's."

That night, Amberley said her prayers as Brenda listened in thoughtfully. They turned out the lights and slid under the crisp white sheets. The stars were bright, and a cool breeze came through the screened window.

"Amber, are you asleep?"

"What is it?" Amberley whispered as she turned to face Brenda.

"Do you think Grandma Andrews will like me? I mean, I never knew my grandparents." Brenda's voice was solemn and a little shaky.

"What's not to like? Dad and Ma love you, I love you, even Billy Gussette loves you—Brenna!"

They both giggled until Ma called up the stairs for them to "get to sleep." They buried their faces in their pillows to muffle their laughter.

When they had ceased laughing, Brenda whispered again. "I know you all love me, but I can't help feeling like a stray cat that has wandered onto your porch. I know you say that God loves me too, but I can't understand why."

"None of us can understand God's love. But He loved us enough to send His Son, the Lord Jesus, to die for us and save us." Amberley sat up a little in bed, hoping that Brenda would be ready to talk more.

"Goodnight, Amber," Brenda said after a long pause. "We'll talk more about it later."

Fifteen
Grandma Andrews and the Big Farm

As the eastern sky hinted of crimson and the grass and flowers were sopping with dew, the girls were up and helping Dad silently pack everything they would need into his pickup truck.

Ma was busy in the kitchen preparing a quick breakfast. A tray of golden brown buttermilk biscuits sat on the counter, fresh from the oven, and a bowl of milk gravy sat on the table

"I don't know what the rich folks eat, Mary, but it certainly can't touch this," Dad said as he bowed his head to pray, waiting for the girls to do the same.

Brenda picked at her food and was quiet as they all began to eat.

"What is it, dear? Don't you feel well?" Ma asked.

"I'm fine, Ma, really I am."

Dad reached over and patted Brenda's shoulder.

"Brenda, when I first went into the army, everything was terribly strange. One day I was a kid in high school, and the next I was wearing a green uniform and being ordered about by drill sergeants. But after the months and years had passed, I was comfortable with army life, and it was hard for me to remember a time when I hadn't been in the service. I think what I'm trying to say is that we all love you here, and soon you will feel like you fit in. The strangeness will fade away, and you will hardly remember a time when you weren't our girl."

Brenda smiled when she heard Dad refer to her as "our girl."

With breakfast over, Dad and the girls finished loading up the truck. He and Ma sat in the front seat, and Brenda and Amberley snuggled among the quilts and blankets in the back. Dad had built wooden sideboards for his pickup truck and covered the top with a green tarpaulin in case it rained. The girls felt like two rabbits hiding in a pen.

The truck rolled through the quiet, lonely village of Sodus. The red and green lights shone along the railroad tracks. The IGA was dark, and only a few cars had arrived at the fruit exchange. The cool, damp air swirled under the canvas tarp, and satisfied with Ma's good breakfast, the girls were soon lulled into sleep.

* * *

Marian Andrews had been up for hours, seeing to the feeding of the stock and the milking of the cows. She loved the early morning hours before sunrise. It was over forty years ago that she and Richard Andrews had set up housekeeping on his father's old farm in Hipps Hollow. It had seemed like a vast wilderness to her at the time, a whole quarter section, but much of the old farm had been sold off. Now, with her husband's passing, she was alone except for Jeb, the hired man, who lived in a small cabin beside the big barn.

The milk truck had arrived to take the cold, thick milk back to Producers Creamery in Benton Harbor to be made into butter, cheese, and ice cream. Jeb, who had been with them over twenty years, herded the black-and-white Holsteins out to pasture. In the early darkness, their black color was invisible, and from a distance in the soft light the cows appeared to be a series of floating white clouds.

The fowls began to stir with the roosters' crowing, a reminder that the eggs had to be gathered for market. Marian rang the brass dinner bell mounted on a pole next to the back porch to signal Jeb that she was ready to discuss the day's activities. He washed his hands and face at the pump and took a seat on the top step. Marian draped a clean hand towel over his arm.

"Here, Jeb," she said, handing him a plate of hot food and a cup of coffee. He eagerly shoveled down the mound of crispy brown fried potatoes and eggs fried sunny-side up. He then took the juicy sausage patties, fragrant with sage, and sandwiched them between several buttermilk biscuits. Marian refilled his coffee cup as he sopped up the yokes on his plate with a remaining bit of biscuit.

"Jeb, I want you to dress three young cockerels, first thing, before you gather the eggs. Sam and Mary will be here shortly, and I want everything to be right for dinner."

"Yes, Miss Marian," he said, licking his fingers.

With the chores caught up for now, Marian washed at the hand pump and scurried into the large farmhouse kitchen that was emblazoned with light. She set dough on to rise in a bowl above the great black cast-iron stove. Soon there would be several golden-brown loaves of bread. She peeled apples and cut rhubarb for pies.

The bright morning sun seemed to trigger a symphony of activities and sounds on the farm. A flock of Canada geese rose from the marshy ground below the hill by the river. A herd of deer came close to forage with the cattle. The chickens began to cluck and scratch in the barnyard with the ducks and turkeys.

Dad drove down the dusty gravel road that led to Grandma's farm. As he turned into the long driveway, Amberley announced loudly, "We're here!"

Brenda could feel her stomach tighten as the truck came to a dusty stop. She had heard Ma and Amberley tell stories about Grandma Andrews. She was very stern and "no-nonsense."

Ma had told them about the time when Grandma was feeding a kitchen full of hired hands and they wouldn't go back to work. Grandma had emptied a box of Grandpa's shotgun shells into the potbellied stove that was blazing red behind them. Some of the men had just come back from the War, and they "lit out like scared cats" when the shells began to explode.

Brenda was worried. Perhaps Grandma would not like her, and in her boldness, would be obvious about it. Brenda remembered how tough she had been before she met the Bridges. She could meet any situation head-on and not care a snap about the consequences. But now she had been allowed to become part of a great family, and she so wanted to fit in.

Dad and Amberley began to carry the bags into the house as Grandma came down the steps. She kissed Dad and Amberley and then Ma. Grandma's hair was snow-white and fixed in a tight bun. She wore thin-rimmed glasses that rested on the middle of her nose. This allowed her to look over her glasses, and she would habitually tilt her head forward when talking. Her dress was a thin, light cotton, patterned with blue flowers. She wore a long apron that hung over her neck and covered almost to her knees.

Grandma spoke with Ma and then turned to Brenda. Brenda stood by the truck, feeling very small even though she was almost as tall as Ma. Grandma approached the girl and reached down to hold both of her hands.

"So, this is Brenda. My, you're a pretty one. With all this red hair around here, I'm kinda glad to see some other

111

color. I want you to know that I'm your grandma, same as with Amberley."

Grandma tenderly drew Brenda to her and whispered in her ear. "I know about your troubles, child. I was so happy when Mary and Sam wanted to take you in. They sent me your picture, and I suppose I loved you before I ever laid eyes on you."

Grandma squeezed Brenda tightly and kissed her gently on the cheek. She took her long apron and wiped away Brenda's tears and her own.

"Now come, child, let's go in the house and get you settled."

Amberley and Brenda carried their bags up to the big attic room on the third floor. This had been Ma's room when she was a young girl and still lived with Grandpa and Grandma Andrews. It was very large and painted a light blue. The ceiling was almost ten feet high with an old bronze chandelier that had been converted from gas to electric many years before. Brenda remarked on how large the old farmhouse was.

"It must have been lonely here without any other children."

"Oh no, Brenda," Amberley replied. "This grand old house was alive with people! Ma had three sisters and four brothers. When Ma was a baby she had a brother in high school. She had this room on the third floor because she was the youngest."

"Wow! Imagine having eight children running around," Brenda laughed.

"The book of Psalms says: 'Lo, children are an heritage of the Lord: and the fruit of the womb is his reward. As arrows are in the hand of a mighty man; so are children of the youth. Happy is the man that hath his quiver full of them.' Large families have always been considered a blessing from God."

Amberley pointed to a large framed photograph on the wall over the bed. "See? Here is a picture of Ma's brothers and sisters with Grandpa and Grandma Andrews."

"Didn't Ma want a large family?" asked Brenda.

"I have two little brothers in heaven, you know. The doctor said that Ma couldn't have any more children. That is, until God sent you to us."

Amberley grew silent and Brenda thoughtful. "Let's finish making these beds," Amberley said. "We can put our clothes in that old maple wardrobe in the corner."

Together, they stood gazing through the big round window that faced the vast acreage of the farm. The huge gable that was their room jutted out into the air and gave them a unique vantage. The fields and orchards seemed to roll on forever. They could see the woods that covered the bleak hollow and the beautiful shimmering river just beyond.

"I could sit here all day and enjoy the view," Brenda

said.

"So could I," said Amberley, "but we won't be able to sit anywhere for very long. Grandma won't tolerate idleness, especially from two strong young girls. I'm surprised she hasn't called us already. If there is any doubt in your mind whether she considers you her granddaughter, wait till she puts you to work."

"Girls!" Grandma's high-pitched voice carried up two flights of stairs. "Don't dawdle! There's work to be done."

"See what I mean?" Amberley laughed. "We're in for it now."

Grandma Andrews stood at the bottom of the stairs and handed each of the girls an apron as they came down.

"Wash up, girls, and help me in the kitchen. There are pies to be made and chickens to fry. After dinner, I'll have Jeb hitch up the buggy, and Amber can show Brenda around the farm."

The girls made the pie dough under Grandma's watchful eye. They were warned about having the exact quantities of flour and fat. "The mixture must be coarse. Add the ice water slowly, a tablespoon at a time."

Grandma then showed the girls how to roll out the dough. "Be careful not to work the dough too much or it will get warm and fall apart. Now heap the sliced apples and cut rhubarb in their shells—don't worry, the fruit will cook down. Always use Jonathan apples, never Delicious. They are too sweet for pies."

As Amberley sprinkled flour, spices, sugar, and chunks of butter to complete the filling, Brenda carefully fitted the crusts in place. She surprised everyone by making fancy leaves out of the leftover dough to decorate the tops.

"My goodness, child, that will look too fancy to eat. I didn't realize you were so talented," Grandma said.

Brenda smiled and blushed as the pies were set in the big oven to bake. Now it was time to cut up the chickens Jeb had dressed. Ma wanted to help, but Grandma wouldn't hear of it.

"The girls are doing fine, Mary. We're not doing them or their future husbands any favors by doing the work for them. Everyone needs to know their way around the kitchen. You know, your brothers are mighty fine cooks."

Brenda set the chicken on to fry while Grandma showed them how to make wilted lettuce. They cut up bacon into small pieces and fried it crisp. Then a little vinegar was mixed into the bacon with the hot drippings and poured over a big pan of fresh leaf lettuce from the garden. The lettuce wilted and made a delicious salad.

Sam had finished helping Jeb with an electrical problem in the cattle barn and returned to the house for a cup of coffee.

"Pull up a seat, Sam. I grind my own beans, you know," Grandma said.

"Thanks, Ma," he said.

While the chicken sizzled in the large cast-iron pan,

Amberley busied herself by keeping up with the dishes. The kitchen was bright and sunny, larger than their whole downstairs in Sodus. Grandma kept it painted bright yellow because Grandpa had believed that happy homes should have yellow kitchens. It was like the sunrise.

Amberley missed Grandpa terribly, but she knew they would see him again in heaven. On his deathbed, he had made everyone promise to meet him there. She smiled and wiped away a tear with her dusty floured hand.

Amberley and Brenda set the table in the large dining room as Grandma rang the dinner bell for Jeb. He was busy in the pasture dropping off bales of hay for the cattle. He had regularly taken his meals in the house with the other hands when Grandpa was still alive, but now he only ate inside on special occasions.

"How is Jeb getting along these days, Ma?" Sam asked Grandma Andrews.

"Oh, he seems to be doing all right. I wish he didn't have to live by himself, but it wouldn't look right for him to be staying here in the house alone with me. I try to make sure he eats right, though," she said.

Since Grandpa had died, production on the farm had been cut down to what Grandma and Jeb could comfortably handle. Grandma was very fond of Jeb. He and Grandpa had been good friends, and Jeb's wife and baby boy were buried next to Grandpa on the orchard hill. Grandma had put in her will that Jeb would get sixty acres on a corner lot when she passed away. But true to Grandma's character, she scolded him regularly. "But don't you start counting your acres before they're hatched, Jeb Sanders. I don't plan on going anywhere for quite a while!"

The girls hurried to change into their work clothes after dinner. Jeb had the horse and buggy waiting for them by the barn. Brenda was a little nervous because she had never seen a horse up close.

"Oh, Amber, I don't know about this," she said as they approached the horse. "I've heard about horses biting off people's ears and such."

"Come here, Brenda. Gray is as tame as a lamb," Amberley said, gently taking Brenda's hand and stroking the horse's nose. "See, he won't hurt you. He likes you."

Brenda smiled. The horse was so gentle that she wasn't afraid to feed him some sugar cubes. Then Gray nuzzled up to Brenda's face and closed his eyes as she scratched the place between his ears.

Grandma had named the horse Gray because he was a dusty gray color. He was a four-year-old stallion born on the farm, and Grandma would often have him pull the buggy to town for groceries on nice days.

Amberley was an old hand at driving the buggy. She and Brenda sat back and let Gray take the well-worn path that he knew well. He kicked up several pheasants that exploded into the air, but he never missed a step. He seemed to enjoy pulling the buggy through Grandma's

117

wilderness.

"It is such a beautiful day," Amberley said. "Later on when it gets warmer, I'll take you to meet Andy and Sarah Buckles in Buckles Hollow."

"Who are the Buckles?" Brenda asked.

Amberley pointed eastward up the river.

"Up there about a half-mile is Buckles Hollow. The Buckles are a very old black couple who have lived there for probably sixty or seventy years. No one knows exactly how old they are. The farmers kind of look in on them from time to time. Sarah is such a sweetheart. You would like her."

Amberley was anxious for Brenda to see the hollow and the river. It was so deep and dark. Grandpa had once told her that the hollow hadn't changed much from the time when the Potawatomi Indians had lived there. He had shown her some arrowheads and spear points he had found there when he was a little boy. There was even an Indian graveyard at the edge of the farm on River Road.

"This place was very special to them, and I aim to keep it just the way it is," Grandpa had told her.

Gray stopped at the edge of the river to drink, and the girls stepped out. The air was almost chilly within the acres and acres of trees.

"See those trees yonder?" Amberley pointed. "Grandpa Andrews said they were several hundred years old. A man from a furniture factory offered him thousands of dollars for them, but Grandpa told him no."

A red-tailed hawk was scolding them from a high branch when Brenda touched Amberley's arm.

"Wait a minute! Do you smell smoke?"

Amberley stood still for a moment as the unmistakable sooty odor of burning pine wood drifted past them. As they hurried back to the buggy, they were shocked at what they saw. There along the shore of the river were footprints—but not the prints left by shoes. These prints were of bare feet, and they meandered back and forth along the muddy shoreline as if they belonged to someone who was lost. The prints were small and light like those of a child.

"Let's go get Dad," Amberley whispered as they turned the buggy back to the farmhouse.

Sixteen
The China Doll

Sam drove the pickup truck back to the river by himself. He was gone for over an hour, and when he returned, he went straight to the telephone. He called the sheriff and told him he had better come out right away.

"What is it, Sam?" Mary asked.

He turned to the girls and said, "How about fetching me some coffee?"

"Both of us, Dad?" Amberley asked.

"Yes. One of you get the coffee and the other one get the cup."

Brenda and Amberley looked at each other. This was Dad's way of telling them to leave the room. Something serious had happened, and he wanted to talk to Ma and Grandma alone.

When Sheriff Warner arrived, he and Sam took the pickup truck because the police car could not navigate over the rough woods road with its ruts and rock outcroppings.

About an hour later, the pickup returned from the dismal hollow. Amberley had been watching for it intently from a chair on the back porch. As Dad and the sheriff slammed the truck doors, she could see that their clothes were filthy with black soot. They stopped to wash their hands and faces at the pump before entering the kitchen door.

"Marian," the sheriff said with a grim face, "may I use your phone?" Grandma said nothing, but she waved her hand toward the phone on the wall. Amberley entered after her father and stood with Brenda behind the chair where Ma was seated, waiting for him to explain the mystery. Dad was silent as he poured coffee for himself and the sheriff. He sat down at the kitchen table and thoughtfully stirred his cup. It was clear that he was in no hurry to speak.

Amberley said nothing, but in her mind she was yelling, *Daddy, what . . . what . . . what?*

"Apparently," he began, "a poor family has been living in the hollow. It's so big and winding that they went unnoticed. They built a shelter out of sticks and old boards that had washed down the hollow and covered it with pine branches. Well, it's been dry, and you know how fast pine needles burn."

Dad paused and reached out to touch Ma's hand. "It looks as if their little hut caught fire last night, and they weren't able to escape. I found the man and woman still inside."

"Oh, dear!" Ma said, leaning forward and putting her hand on Dad's arm.

121

Amberley looked at the ashes and soot on Dad's hands and clothes and thought of the horrible things her father had just seen. He was a big, strong, brave man, but it was clear by his somber mood that the incident had affected him. She moved to Dad's side and put her arm around his shoulder. The smell of the ashes and oily pine soot was heavy around him, and it reminded her of what she and Brenda had smelled in the hollow. Suddenly, she remembered the footprints on the bank of the river. The footprints of a little child!

"But what about the child, Dad?" Amberley asked.

"There was no child, Amber, only two adults."

"But the footprints we saw by the river belonged to a little child!"

Dad set his cup down hard, spilling his coffee. "Girls, quickly! Go get Jeb."

Brenda and Amberley rushed out the back door to the barn. Sam turned to the sheriff, who had just gotten off the phone.

"Sheriff Warner, I think we might have a little child wandering around in a hundred acres of dark woods. If you can, get some more men and a dog. Jeb and I will go back out there now and start looking."

* * *

Late into the night, the searchers combed the dark,

cold woods of Hipps Hollow. Grandma and Mary kept hot coffee brewing and hot food ready for the worn-out men. Grandma had made a large roast to cut up for hot roast-beef-and-gravy sandwiches. "The men need something that will stick to their ribs," she said.

As the weary night waned, the disappointed men still had not found the child. The tracking dog seemed to pick up the child's scent, but then it became confused and wandered about in circles. No matter where they found the trail in the woods, the dog ended up at the river's edge, giving forth the saddest howl. Sam and the sheriff were afraid that the child must have drowned. If that were so, there was nothing more that could be done.

Sam stood with the sheriff, peering out over the St. Joseph River. Its rushing water crackled along the bank on its journey west to Lake Michigan. The spring peepers chirped loudly in unison throughout the hollow, and the occasional smallmouth bass leaped at the swarms of mayflies, landing on the surface of the water with a loud flop.

"I don't think anything could get too far down the river before getting hung up on the sandbars below. We'll start our search there and work our way back upriver as soon as the boat and diving equipment get here in the morning," the sheriff said.

The tired men returned to the house to eat and then go home. Amberley and Brenda had been curled up in their blankets on Grandma's big couch, and they stirred with the noise of the men talking in the kitchen. Amberley heard her father say that "The mission has turned from one of rescue to a recovery operation." She figured this meant they had given up hope of finding the child alive.

When the sheriff and his men finally left, the girls went into the kitchen with their blankets wrapped about them. Dad was seated at the table with Ma and Grandma. Amberley looked at her father, who was so dirty and tired. She was concerned about him and what he had to do in the morning. She knew he would be one of the searchers—he had learned to be an expert diver while in the Special Forces. This would not be the first time he'd had to do this sad but necessary task.

Brenda reached for her hand and squeezed it, and Amberley exchanged a sad glance with her mother. Even Grandma had tears in her eyes. They were all so weary and sad about the unfortunate people who were so poor that they had to live—and die—in Grandma's woods. Dad washed his face and hands in the kitchen sink and sat down in a comfortable chair in the living room to get a few hours of sleep.

"If I had only known, I could have done something," Grandma said sadly. "Oh, how pitiful! How pitiful!"

Before Dad closed his eyes, he pulled a dirty, burnt envelope out of his pocket. Inside were several blue and green bills of paper money and some coins. He handed it to his wife.

"What is this, Sam?"

"This is all they had in the world—South Vietnamese piasters. They are totally worthless."

"My, how pretty and colorful. To think this came from that war-torn land," Ma said thoughtfully.

"Evidently, they came here from Vietnam to start a new life and somehow ended up in the woods. There was evidence they had been living off the land. We found fish bones and the like around their camp. I don't know what they expected to do once winter came. Perhaps they did not know about our winters. But now—now all of their dreams are gone in a few moments of time. Now the apple of their eye is perhaps at the bottom of the river."

The girls gave their father a quick kiss on their way to bed. As they started up the stairs, he called them back. "Girls?"

"What is it, Dad?" Amberley asked. He held out his arms and said, "Give us a hug."

The girls cuddled up next to him and kissed him. They tried to understand what he must be feeling. Thinking of the poor little child who had wandered off into the night must have made him feel closer to his own children.

* * *

The next morning was gray and rainy. A storm front

125

had moved in during the night, and this would only make it more difficult for the men. The hollow and the river were dark enough even when there was plenty of sunshine.

Brenda helped Ma make breakfast, though it was a cheerless morning. They would be eating out of habit rather than from hunger.

"We had better plan on making food and coffee for the men when they get here. It's no telling how long this is going to take," Grandma said. She turned to Brenda and Amberley. "I hope you know what a fine and brave pa you have there."

Ma smiled. "This is the man I truly married. He was hiding for awhile, that's all."

Amberley hugged her mother with a tear in her eye. "I know, Ma. I can see that now." The puzzled look on Brenda's face made it evident that she did not understand. She had not been privy to Dad's former life. Someday they would tell her, and it might help her to understand how gracious the Lord had been to them all.

"Thank the Lord for both of your parents," Grandma said.

Amberley smiled. "And thank the Lord for you, Grandma."

Grandma blushed. Amberley was surprised—she had never seen her blush before. "Oh, nonsense!" Grandma said.

Dad stirred from his chair, and brushing his hair back

with his hand, he sat down at the kitchen table. Ma poured his coffee.

"The sheriff will be here soon with a boat and equipment. If you would rather go home, Mary, and take the girls?"

"I'd rather stay here and help you and Mom," she said.

"Of course you would," he said. "I wasn't thinking."

Grandma stood looking out the screen door. The morning was still except for a few geese circling the river in search of a landing place. The rain was soft and gentle. *Barring the sad business at hand,* she thought, *it is a rare morning to be alive.*

"I wonder what's got Jeb all in a fuss?" she said.

Jeb was hobbling toward the farmhouse. His bad knee always caused him to limp when the weather was wet.

"Miss Marian! Miss Marian! It's uh china doll! Come see the china doll!"

"Bless the man, what's he talking about?" Grandma exclaimed.

Amberley remembered that Grandma had once remarked that Jeb wasn't the "sharpest knife in the drawer" and that he had a difficult time explaining himself, especially when he was agitated. She could see the truth of that now!

"China doll, Miss Marian, in the barn!"

They all followed Jeb to the barn, ignoring the rain. He took his lantern off a nail and led them to the corner of a

127

straw-filled manger. Amberley leaned forward, peering around Dad for a better look. There, sleeping in the warm dry straw, was a little girl. She was dressed in dusty black pajamas. Her hair was as black as Brenda's, and her runny nose and tears had dried on her cheeks. She had pretty almond-shaped eyes and olive skin. It was obvious that this was the lost child of the Vietnamese family in the woods.

"Oh, dear Lord!" Ma exclaimed. "Pick her up at once, Sam. Don't let her be out in this weather a second longer."

Dad gently picked up the dirty and exhausted little girl in his big arms. She was still asleep, but she instinctively put her tiny arms around Dad's neck.

Amberley saw the tears begin to well up in Dad's eyes. He gently carried the little one into the house, and Ma drew a warm bath. When the little "china doll" opened her eyes, she did not cry or look surprised. She hung onto Dad's neck tightly and refused to let go when Ma tried to take her to the bath.

"I wonder she doesn't cry," Grandma said.

"If she's been through one fraction of what her people have suffered, there are no more tears to cry," Dad said. "Let her rest in my arms for a spell, and then we will see to her bath."

Then Amberley was surprised when Dad spoke to the little girl in her own language. She knew he had been a Green Beret in Vietnam, but she had never heard him speak Vietnamese.

The little girl's face lit up as she answered his questions in her own strange tongue. Amberley watched her dad and the little girl conversing back and forth, sometimes using their hands for expression. At that moment, she was so proud of him.

Finally, the little girl began to weep. Dad tenderly hugged her to his neck, saying to her in her language, "It is enough."

Dad looked around at his eagerly waiting family and began to speak. "She tells me that her parents moved here from Vietnam to start a better life for themselves. A bad man in Chicago who was supposed to help them tricked them and took all of their money. They hitched a ride on a truck and were dumped off here in Sodus Township."

Dad paused to comfort Lien, patting her gently on the back. "They hid out during the day and walked only at night until they found a place in Grandma's woods. Her father didn't know who the woods belonged to, but they reminded him of the dark jungle in Vietnam. They were all very homesick."

Amberley and Brenda were wide-eyed as they listened to the amazing story. Ma and Grandma only sniffed back tears.

"Her father was a fisherman, so they were able to live off the river. But soon they ran out of matches and had to keep a fire burning all the time for cooking. That's apparently when the dry pine boughs on the hut caught fire in the middle of the night. She says the last thing she remembers is her father throwing her clear of the blazing hut and yelling at her to run and not look back. She says she was terrified last night when she saw the lights in the woods and heard the men talking and the dog howling. She just walked around and around in circles in the dark and somehow ended up in the big barn."

"That's why the dog couldn't pick up her trail, I'll bet!" Amberley said. "What's her name, Dad, and how old is she?"

Dad spoke to her again in Vietnamese.

"She's seven years old, but she certainly doesn't look older than five. She says her name is Lien Huong. 'Huong' refers to the fragrance of flowers, if I remember right."

Ma stood up from her chair. "Enough questions for now, Sam. Let's get her washed up and into clean clothes. Mom thinks she might have some of my old clothes in a barrel in the attic."

Lien allowed Ma to give her a bath, and Grandma put her in one of Ma's old sleeping gowns. Now that the little girl was fresh and clean and her shiny black hair was combed, she truly did resemble a beautiful china doll. Grandma sat her down at the table to eat. She was so hungry that she began stuffing the food in her tiny mouth with both hands. Ma quickly grabbed both her arms to slow her down.

"Not too fast, honey, or it will come right back up

again. There's no need to rush. I will see to it that you will never lack for food or warmth again." Ma cooed and smiled at Lien to make the little girl understand that there was plenty of food and plenty of time to eat it.

Dad contacted the sheriff on the phone. "Sheriff, we have good news. Jeb found the child sleeping in the barn. She's a little girl and seems to be in good health." Dad paused, "Yes, sir, I am too."

Dad hung up the phone. "The sheriff was so relieved. He told me that all he could think about was his little seven-year-old granddaughter."

His face grew somber. "Mary, we have another problem here," he said, looking at Lien.

"What, Sam?" Ma answered, wiping the breakfast off Lien's face and hands.

"She still doesn't realize what has happened to her folks. We have to tell her right away."

Ma plopped down in the chair next to Lien. The look on her face showed that she had not thought of that. Lien had been so cold, dirty, and frightened that she could not think past her hunger and exhaustion. The little girl who sat in their bright and cheery kitchen had no clue that she was now an orphan.

"Look at her, Mary. She's so tired that she can't even hold her head up. Put her to bed for now. It will give me time to pray for a way to tell her that her mother and father won't be coming back."

131

* * *

The long summer was over, and September had come. Amberley and Brenda were back in school, and with them went little Lien. The courts had asked the Bridges to be foster parents for Lien until someone could adopt her. They wholeheartedly agreed. The girls had spent the summer trying to teach her enough English so that she might start Sodus School that fall. She was learning fast, but her English was pidgin at best. Miss Sullivan considered Lien her special project and patiently worked with her every day.

Earlier that summer, the Bridges had been summoned to court to speak with a judge about Brenda. They learned that at Mr. Bickel's hearing, he had agreed to give up all custody rights to Brenda as his daughter. The prosecutor told him that if he would leave the state and not ever come back, they would drop all charges.

The judge took Brenda into his chambers and told her what her father had agreed to. He asked Brenda if she wanted to go with her father or stay with Mr. and Mrs. Bridges.

Brenda spoke softly. "I know that my father never loved me. He told me so almost every day. He said I was an unwanted mistake and that he would have left me in a raspberry patch if Mom hadn't made him promise to take care of me. I have not been happier since I came to live with

132

the Bridges. I know they love me, because they tell me so all the time. If they want me, I would like to stay with them forever."

The hard, stern old judge called the Bridges into his chambers and excused himself for a moment to get something out of his eye. When he returned, he spoke to them.

"Mr. and Mrs. Bridges, if you are agreeable, and I believe you are, I find Mr. Bickel an unfit parent and give you permanent custody of Brenda as her foster parents. If at such time in the future you elect to proceed with permanent adoption, please see me personally, and I will help you all I can."

Sam spoke up. "Your honor, Mrs. Bridges and I have fallen in love with Brenda and already consider her our daughter. Our other girl, Amberley, loves her as a sister. If Brenda would agree, we would like to adopt her right away."

Then Sam turned to Brenda. "Honey? We have already talked it over and have agreed that if you want to be our daughter, we would love for you to be part of our family."

Brenda started to cry. "I would like that very much," she said. The stern old judge, who seemed to have gotten something in his eye again, cleared his throat and told the Bridges that he would "get the ball rolling." Brenda Bickel would soon become Brenda Bridges.

* * *

On a cold and rainy October night, as the wind raced and tree branches scraped against the window glass, the Bridges sat inside their bright and cozy living room. Sam read the paper while Amberley and Brenda studied their homework. Mary sat silently knitting and watching as Lien played with a new doll. She had grown to love the little girl. Suddenly, Mary broke the silence of the moment.

"Sam, let's adopt Lien, too!"

The girls looked up at their mother with their mouths wide open.

Sam smiled and folded his paper. "I'm afraid you're too late, Mary."

Mary dropped her knitting, and the ball of yarn rolled off her lap. "Oh Sam! We've waited too long, and now someone has beat us to it!"

Sam chuckled. "What I meant was that *you* are too late. I've already looked into the matter. I spoke with the judge who helped us with our Brenda, and he says it looks pretty promising."

Mary leaped from her chair and covered Sam's face with hugs and kisses.

"Oh Sam, I love you so much!"

Amberley and Brenda looked at each other and smiled. Lien smiled, too. She did not understand what was being said, but she could tell it was something good.

"Well, I see it this way." Sam said. "We were not able to have all the children we wanted the natural way, so the Lord fixed it so we could make a home for Brenda and little Lien. And we do love them as much as if they were born to us."

Sam called Lien up on his lap and asked her in Vietnamese if she would like to come and live with them and be their daughter. Her answer was easily understood by all. She smiled and cuddled up against Sam's neck and kissed him.

"Well," Amberley said, "let's welcome another stray cat."

Seventeen
The New Judge

Mary sat at the kitchen table, peering out the window at the swirling snow. A late November snowstorm had frosted everything white, and she was concerned about the girls who would be walking home from school.

Thanksgiving was next week, and Mary was happy because she had won a twenty-five-pound turkey from the IGA in a drawing. Grandma Andrews and even Jeb would be coming for dinner this year, and everyone was contemplating the wonderful holiday.

Mary thought of all the changes that had occurred in her life in such a short time—Sam's salvation and Brenda and Lien becoming part of the family.

I want so desperately to see Brenda saved, but she always seems to shy away when I mention it, she thought. *And there is Lien. Sam could speak to her in Vietnamese, but would she understand at her young age?*

Mary could feel the great weight of the girls' salvation pressing on her shoulders as she bowed her head to pray for them.

136

* * *

Amberley and Brenda bundled up little Lien for the bitter walk home from Sodus School. Most of her seven years had been spent in a steamy hot jungle village in Vietnam. Cold and snow were new to her, but she seemed to thoroughly enjoy this strange weather that she had only heard about in stories.

Brenda smiled as she pulled the ends of Lien's coat sleeves over her mittens, but she couldn't help feeling a sense of worry. The Bridges were waiting for the court to approve the adoption of Lien. The kind old judge who had helped them adopt Brenda had told them that he would do everything in his power to make it happen as quickly as possible. But Dad thought they should have heard something by now.

"Let us di di," Lien said. Lien was learning English at a rapid pace, but she frequently mixed her English and Vietnamese words and phrases together. The girls knew that "di di" was Lien's way of saying "Let's go!"

The three girls braced themselves to begin the walk home. The wind was blowing in tremendous gusts that rattled even the heavy windows of the school building. As the unseen hand of the wind slammed the door shut behind them, they heard a horn honking out front.

The girls squealed with delight to see Dad's old

pickup truck. It was very old and faded green. It had been painted years ago with a paintbrush and looked horrible. Amberley knew that they could not afford a brand new truck but Dad was still proud of it anyway.

"Would you girls like a ride?" Dad shouted through the window.

Brenda picked up Lien, and she and Amberley fought the stinging snow to Dad's truck and quickly pulled the door shut behind them. Lien sat on Brenda's lap and instinctively leaned over to give Dad a hug and kiss. She spoke to him in Vietnamese, and he answered, "I'm glad to see you too, sweetheart."

When they arrived at home, Brenda opened the back door of the kitchen, and Amberley quickly closed it behind Lien and Dad. Ma was heating milk on the stove for hot chocolate. "I'm so glad you picked up the girls, Sam."

"I'll be right back. I have some things in the truck," Dad said.

"How did Lien do today in school, girls?"

"Great, Ma," Amberley said. "Everyone just loves her. Miss Sullivan works with her on English, and she is learning so fast that I'll bet she speaks fluently by spring."

"Well, that may be a little ambitious, but I am pleased she is doing so well."

"I write all my family name," Lien said, proudly holding up a sheet of paper. Miss Sullivan had taught her how to write the names of Amberley, Brenda, Sam and

Mary Bridges, and even Grandma Andrews.

"That's wonderful, honey. I'll put that on the refrigerator," Ma said, taking the paper from her.

Then Lien's face grew serious. "Why my name not Bridges, my mother?"

Brenda and Amberley glanced at each other. Ma opened her mouth to speak.

"Sweetie . . ."

Just then, Dad came through the door with a whoosh. He had the mail and a bag of groceries in his arm.

"Finally, a letter from the courts, Mary," he said, holding the letter up for her to see.

"Oh, read it, Sam. Maybe it's news about Lien."

Dad opened the envelope and scanned the letter. His smile quickly turned to disgust as he slammed the letter down on the kitchen table. Everyone looked up in surprise.

"What is it, Sam?" Ma said.

"Pencil-pushing bureaucrats!" Dad said angrily.

Dad looked down at Lien, who had formed the most pitiful look on her face. She meekly put her arms down to her sides and looked up at him with a sideways glance. She had never heard him raise his voice in anger before. He quickly composed himself and reached down to pull her close to him.

"Girls, please take Lien up to your room. I'll call you when supper is ready," Ma said.

Amberley took Lien by the hand, and Brenda followed

139

them out of the room. As the girls began to ascend the stairs, Brenda paused on the bottom step. "Amber," she whispered. "you go on up. I'll be there in a moment."

Brenda quickly found a place of vantage against the wall and listened intently to her parents' conversation in the kitchen. Ma picked the letter up off the table and began to read it aloud.

"Dear Mr. and Mrs. Bridges," it said,

> This is regarding your application to adopt Lien Huong, an alleged orphan from Vietnam. Due to the international nature and implications of this case, jurisdiction has now been referred to Judge Emily Richardson, a federal judge in Grand Rapids, who has ordered a complete investigation to determine if Lien Huong has relatives still living in Vietnam. It is the opinion of Judge Richardson that the welfare of the child would be best served if she were returned to her own people. If it is determined that she has family still living in her country of origin, an order will be issued for her repatriation.

Ma could no longer contain herself and began to weep openly. Brenda was ashamed at herself for eavesdropping, but she had needed to know about Lien. *Could I be given back just as easily?* she thought. Brenda quietly reentered the kitchen and put her arms around Ma, fighting back her own tears. "Honey, you shouldn't eavesdrop," Ma said, but she reached up to touch Brenda's arm. "Go now," she said, and Brenda reluctantly obeyed.

"We need to get a lawyer. I'm not giving up on this without a good fight!" Dad said.

Ma wiped her tears on her apron. "Sam—before we do anything else, let's pray about this thing. If we are ever going to see little Lien grow up into a fine Christian lady, we need to get the Lord's help and wisdom."

Dad and Ma sat at the kitchen table as the storm raged outside. Dad began to pray.

"Dear Lord Jesus, chances are this little girl you have given us will grow up in a godless heathen land if you don't intervene in her behalf. Her father and mother brought her here to live in America where she could take advantage of our bounty. You have given her to us; please don't take her away."

Dad said nothing more. He kissed Ma on the cheek and bundled himself up in his hat and coat. "I'll be back in a little while," he said. "I'll be in my work shed."

Brenda had left the kitchen, but she paused at the foot of the stairs to hear Dad's prayer. She quickly ascended the stairs and sat on the edge of her bed.

"What is it, Brenda?" Amberley asked.

Brenda looked at Lien, who was smiling. "Something has gone wrong. A new judge is going to send Lien . . ." Brenda paused. "Amber, why does your family always pray

141

when they get into trouble? Does it ever help?"

Amberley was not prepared for this question, and she remained silent. Brenda stood up. "I'm going downstairs to help Ma with supper. If praying does help—pray for me. The judge might want to send me back too."

As Brenda left the room, Amberley squinted her eyes and thought, *What was that all about?*

As Brenda peeled potatoes over the sink, she wondered how this new judge could possibly think it was better for Lien to go back to Communist Vietnam. Her parents had perished trying to make a better life for their daughter. How could this judge not see that?

* * *

That night, Amberley lay across her bed to do her devotions. She had always prayed and read her Bible in silence so as not to bother Brenda. But tonight, Brenda turned from the wall to face Amberley. "Amber, would you do your devotions out loud tonight; you know, so I could listen?"

Amberley was surprised. "Sure. I usually start out by reading a passage of scripture. Then I think about it and ask the Holy Spirit to apply it to my life and help me understand it."

Brenda was thoughtful. "Who is the Holy Spirit? Is he like an angel or something?"

Amberley held back a smile. "No, the Holy Spirit is God."

She could see that Brenda did not quite understand. "You see, Brenda, there is only one God, but He exists in three Persons: God the Father, God the Son, who is the Lord Jesus Christ, and God the Holy Spirit. When a person accepts the Lord Jesus as his Savior, God the Holy Spirit enters his body and dwells there, making it His temple. One of the things the Holy Spirit does is help us understand the Bible."

Brenda pursed her lips, trying to process what she had just heard.

"Now here is the scripture verse I am going to read tonight," Amberley said after a pause. She read Proverbs 21:1: "The king's heart is in the hand of the Lord, as the rivers of water: he turneth it whithersoever he will."

Brenda's brow was furrowed. "I don't get it. I guess I do need the Holy Spirit to help me with this one." She smiled.

Amberley read the verse again and explained, "This verse says that God is in control of all kings. He is able to control their hearts like someone diverting the flow of a river or stream."

Then Amberley sat up on the edge of her bed. "Brenda, I'm going to claim this verse for little Lien. I am going to pray that the Lord will turn Judge Richardson's heart so that she will let us adopt her."

"But it says 'the king's heart,' Amber. Judge Richardson is not a king."

"The principle is still the same, Brenda. The Lord is in control of all leaders and rulers—even judges." Amberley thought of her own experiences with Miss Collins and how the Lord had mellowed her heart. "The Lord is the only chance of Lien becoming our little sister."

Brenda sat up in her bed. "I can't bear the thought of Lien going back to Vietnam. Everything I have read about the war and what went on over there is horrible." Brenda's eyes grew moist as she thought about how helpless she had felt all of those years living with her father. She thought of his bouts of drinking and how he would hit her and insult her for no reason at all. How she lived at the library, day after day, because she couldn't bear to go home, wondering if it would ever end.

Amberley spoke, breaking Brenda's thread of thought. "Dad told me a few of the things he saw over there when he was in the army. How the Communist soldiers, the Viet Cong, would torture and then murder whole villages. How they would slaughter little children in front of their parents to strike terror into their hearts and control them. I think it would break him, Brenda, if he had to let her go. God must change the judge's heart. He just has to do it!"

Eighteen

Sam Sees a Lawyer

The wind had abated by morning, and it was snowing softly. Sam had an appointment to see Mr. Enkins's lawyer just after lunch. Mr. Enkins was not only Sam's boss, but also a true friend. He took the time off to ride in with Sam to Benton Harbor.

Mary absentmindedly went through the motions of housework that morning, awaiting Sam's return. When she heard his truck pull into the alley, she ran to the door.

"What did he say, Sam?"

Sam's face showed the disappointment he felt. "The lawyer was very empathetic, Mary, but there is very little he can do. Since Lien's parents were in the country illegally, she isn't considered an American citizen and doesn't really have any rights."

"But Sam, why don't they just let us adopt her? She's only one little girl!" Mary shouted.

"Everything was going fine until the State Department got wind of what happened," Sam said, entering the kitchen and tossing the lawyer's business card on the table.

145

"Some official with nothing better to do apparently wants to normalize relations with Vietnam, and they have urged the judge to send her back to her village. The Vietnamese government has declared Lien's parents, criminals and traitors and demanded the little girl be returned immediately. The State Department doesn't want to make waves."

Sam turned to the window and gazed out at the gently falling snow. "And that's not all, Mary. The attorney checked with the court in Grand Rapids while we were there." Sam hesitated. His words came reluctantly. "Judge Richardson has already ordered her return to Vietnam and has set a date."

"Oh, no, Sam! This is going much too fast," Mary exclaimed, rising to her feet. Sam turned and put his arms around his wife. "They will be here to take her next Wednesday, Mary."

"Sam, that's the day before Thanksgiving! Her first Thanksgiving! Oh, how cruel! How absolutely cruel!"

Sam held Mary in his arms as they stood quietly for a long while. Then they prayed together in the stillness of the snowy afternoon and asked the Lord to have His will. The coffee pot steamed and the kitchen clock ticked in the lazy silence of the room as Mary's hand slipped softly into Sam's.

"My little girl," he whispered. "Oh, my little girl."

* * *

Saturday morning was sunny and bright. Amberley and Brenda were going to take Lien sledding down the long hill on Hillandale Road. The girls knew this would probably be the last time they would go sledding with Lien, but they forced themselves to remain cheerful. Ma filled Dad's big thermos bottle with hot chocolate.

"Girls, why don't you see if Billy Gussette wants to go along? I saw his mother yesterday at the IGA, and I know she wishes Billy had more friends."

"That's a good idea, Ma," Amberley replied.

The girls walked down the alley to the Gussettes' house, where Billy and his mother lived all alone. Mr. Gussette had been a sheriff's deputy and was killed during a bank holdup only two days before Christmas. Amberley had heard her mother say that Sharon Gussette was still taking her husband's death very hard even though it had happened over five years ago. Billy did not really remember his father.

Mrs. Gussette worked as a waitress in the evenings, which sometimes left Billy with a sitter. Ma and Mrs. Enkins tried to help her with food and other necessities, but it was rare that she would accept any charity.

Amberley and the girls approached the Gussettes' door and knocked. "Mrs. Gussette, we are going sledding on Chapel Hill. Would Billy like to come with us?"

147

Amberley asked.

"I'm sure he would. Let me get him dressed."

Mrs. Gussette soon arrived at the door, with Billy all bundled up and hardly able to move. His ruddy little face was all that showed.

"Hi, Brenna!" were the first words out of his mouth.

Brenda laughed. "Let's go, Billy."

"Hi, Lee-yan!" Billy said. Lien smiled at the funny little boy she knew from school. Her shiny black hair and olive-brown skin were beautiful in the intensely bright sunshine.

"Boy, you're sure perdy, Lee-yan!" Billy exclaimed. Billy's English was so horrendous that Lien could only hold up her hands to show him that she didn't understand.

"Uh-oh, 'Brenna,' it looks like you're being replaced," Amberley laughed. "How fickle you are, Billy!"

"You're breaking my heart, Billy," Brenda said.

"How come Lee-yan can't talk?" Billy asked.

"Her name is pronounced 'Lee-yen,' Billy," Brenda scolded him mildly. "Don't you remember Miss Sullivan telling the class that she is from a country on the other side of the world called Vietnam? Lien is learning to speak English. Just speak slowly so she can understand you."

"My daddy was a so-ger in Veet'nam." Billy said, hanging his little head. "But he was killed by uh bank robber."

Brenda put her arm tenderly around Billy's shoulders.

148

"Let's go, Billy. We're here to have fun today."

As they arrived at the top of the hill near Edwards Road, Brenda and Amberley took turns watching for traffic. Lien seemed to enjoy playing in the brisk, bitter cold and snow. She enjoyed it most when she was thrown from the sled into a deep drift. After several hours of fun and a few hot chocolate breaks, the sun began to rapidly fall toward the west.

"I wish I could be like Joshua and command the sun to stand still. We're having such a good time," Amberley said.

"I know, and I see that Billy and Lien are becoming good friends. I'm so hurt," Brenda laughed.

Amberley smiled, but her smile quickly faded into true sadness. "I know, and it looks like this might be their last time to play together."

Nineteen
Judge Richardson

After the Sunday morning service, Pastor Mitchell suggested to Sam and Mary that they might speak personally to Judge Richardson about Lien.

"Perhaps if she met you two and Lien, she might have some compassion," he said. "Anyway, it's worth a try."

Sam was able to schedule an appointment with Judge Richardson in Grand Rapids for late Monday morning. Mary called a few trusted friends to pray for them. Before leaving the house, Sam sat Lien down and explained to her the best he could about the judge. He spoke to her in Vietnamese to make certain that she understood.

"Honey, today we are going on a long journey to a big city called Grand Rapids. There is a judge who wants to meet you. She is very wise and powerful, like the chief in your village. We want you to become our daughter, and we must have her permission. Do you understand?"

Lien, with wide eyes, nodded. "Yes, my father."

With that, they began their journey north, not knowing what to expect. They were nervous despite the unusual luxury of their drive—Mr. Enkins had insisted that Sam take his car rather than the old pickup.

After an almost two-hour drive, Lien saw a large valley open up before her, revealing the largest city she had ever seen. She had only known her village in Vietnam before Sodus, and several times she had seen Benton Harbor, but Grand Rapids was like another world to her. Huge tall buildings, blinking lights, and hundreds of cars and trucks were everywhere. Large groups of people walked the streets like ants around an anthill. The streets were filled with the constant honking of car horns and police cars with their blue and red lights. Once, Dad had to slam on his brakes because a beautiful red firetruck raced by. Its siren wailed and its red lights flashed.

Dad parked the car along a street in the heart of this jungle made of stone. Lien watched Ma put a coin in the parking meter. Ma twisted the knob, and it made a whirring sound as the red flag disappeared. Lien watched it earnestly for a few moments, but nothing happened. Ma took her by the hand and whisked her away. Lien glanced back at the meter. *Not even a gum ball,* she thought.

Lien and the Bridges walked for several blocks until they came to the front of a huge building. Lien stopped and looked straight up. She had never seen anything that tall before except for trees and some distant mountains back in Vietnam. Dad and Ma led her through the revolving door, which frightened her. It just turned and turned, and

151

suddenly spit them out inside the building, and before she could recover her senses, a large door opened in the far wall of the lobby.

She tried to read the word "elevator" above it but could not understand the big word. It seemed to be a small room filled with people all facing forward. As the room emptied out, Dad and Ma stood patiently waiting to go in. This was all Lien could take. She shook herself loose from Ma's hand and ran back to the revolving door. She tried to go through it, but it just turned and turned like the huge glass jaws of a dragon, waiting to devour her. Suddenly, someone grabbed her from behind and picked her up. She turned to scream, but there was Dad's smiling face.

Lien began to cry, and she buried her face in Dad's shoulder. She could smell his cologne. It was familiar and reminded her of her secure little world in Sodus.

"We're so sorry, sweetie," Dad said softly. "We didn't think about how new and strange the big city might be to you. Are you okay?"

"Yes, my father," Lien said, face still half buried. "It's just so scary. It's like everything is so big and just wants to swallow me up."

Dad set her down and turned to his wife. "Mary, we have some time. Let's get something to eat and let Lien acclimate to the city."

Dad took Lien's hand, and they walked to the little diner at the other side of the lobby. Dad lifted her up and

152

sat her on a bar stool. It was strange, but she liked it because she could spin around and around.

"Honey?" Ma said. "You're going to get sick and throw up. Don't spin around so much."

The waitress set a blue plate down in front of Lien. There, gloriously before her, was a big juicy hamburger with onions and melting cheese. Heaped in a golden pile were crispy hot French fries and a little paper cup filled with ketchup. Then the waitress returned and set a large stainless steel glass down in front of her. It was tall and covered with frost. Lien sipped from the straw, and her eyes lit up. It was a chocolate malt, so icy cold and sweet. She had never tasted anything so wonderful in all of her life. *I think I might like the big city after all,* she thought with a smile.

Lien's apprehension fled as she rode the elevator to the courtroom floor. It made her stomach feel funny, but she loved it. "Daddy, may we go again?"

"After we meet with the judge, sweetie," he said.

At the appointed time, the Bridges and Lien were shown into the judge's chambers. As they waited on the squeaky leather couch, Lien noticed that the ceiling was very high and the room cold. The walls were covered with wood, which made the room dark and gloomy. A single lamp with a pretty green shade burned brightly on the judge's desk.

Suddenly, a large door seemed to open up out of the

wall. Judge Emily Richardson walked in, and the Bridges stood up. Judge Richardson was very petite and seemed to be lost in the vastness of her robes. She was an older lady, but very pretty. She reminded Lien of her real mother. Her heart warmed. If Judge Richardson was like her mother, then surely she would want what was best for her.

Judge Richardson greeted the Bridges cordially and thanked them for coming. "So, this is little Lien. I've heard so much about her," she said, holding Lien's small hand in her own and offering her some candy from the bowl on her desk. "How may I help you folks?"

Dad spoke first. "Your Honor, thank you for agreeing to meet with us. I believe there has been some undue haste in disposing of this child. Judge Trail was helping us to adopt Lien, and the next thing I know, she's being sent back to Vietnam."

Judge Richardson seemed to stiffen up as the smile fled from her face. "Well, Mr. Bridges, we are not 'disposing' of anyone. I feel, and so does the State Department, that it would be in the little girl's best interest to be with her own people. My contacts tell me that she has grandparents and aunts and uncles in her home village. Don't you think she would be better off with them?"

Lien could not understand all of the big words, but she was not worried. She knew that Dad was a great man. He could do anything. She had known some American soldiers like him in Vietnam. They were kind to her and sometimes gave her candy. Dad would work it out somehow.

Dad stood up and glanced back at Ma and Lien. "Your Honor, I was a Green Beret in the Special Forces and served in Vietnam for over four years. I have seen what the Communists can do to little children. Lien's parents have been branded as traitors. Do you honestly think she will be allowed to have a normal life with that hanging over her head?"

Judge Richardson turned sideways in her chair and fidgeted with an antique wooden gavel that she kept on her desk. "Mr. Bridges, the State Department has been assured by the Vietnamese government that all has been forgiven and that Lien will be given every advantage."

Dad put his hands on the edge of the judge's desk and leaned forward as he spoke.

"Your Honor, will that advantage include growing up in a Christian home with two older sisters and parents who deeply love her? I have seen what happens to the families of people accused of treason in Vietnam. I have seen with my own eyes whole villages tortured and executed because they were just acquaintances of suspected traitors. Do you want to take the chance of this happening to Lien? And have your sources in the State Department confirmed that she still has living relatives, or are they just taking the Vietnamese's word for it?"

Ma spoke up, fighting back tears. "Judge, I know my

husband is telling the truth. After all these years, he still hasn't gotten over what he saw in Vietnam. If you are aware of what happened to her parents, how they died in the fire —please don't make her go through another separation. You have the power, Judge, to save or destroy this little girl's life. Please have mercy on her."

Judge Richardson adjusted her glasses, and Lien noticed that her hand was shaking. Something was wrong, and she wanted to speak to Dad about it, but she did not want to be disrespectful.

"I must do what I think is best for the child," Judge Richardson said emphatically. "How do we know that her parents wanted Lien raised as a Christian? Most of the Vietnamese people are Buddhists, aren't they?"

Dad answered, "Your Honor, I am a Christian. I believe the Bible is the Word of God and the only true instruction book on living and the way to heaven. If I am right, and I believe I am, you are not only condemning Lien to a life of godless Communism but to an eternity in hell."

Lien looked up at Dad, remembering the loud voice she had heard him use in the kitchen. Ma gently touched Dad's arm to remind him that he was speaking with a judge. He looked at her and then sat down. Judge Richardson sat in silence for a few moments before she spoke.

"Mr. and Mrs. Bridges, I am indeed sorry. I must do what I think is right. There is no evidence that Lien will be any better off with you than with her own people. I must ask you to leave now. I have a very busy docket."

Dad and Ma looked at each other with utter helplessness on their faces. Dad picked up Lien, and they left the room. As the revolving courthouse door cast them out onto the sidewalk, the bitter November air brought them back to reality.

The drive back to Sodus seemed to take forever, and they spoke very little. Lien sat between them, thinking about her experiences in the big city. She thought of all the people she had seen, the pretty red firetruck and the delicious chocolate malt. She looked forward to going there again someday.

* * *

The house was quiet when they arrived at home, and the girls were still in school. Sam said nothing as he ascended the stairs to the attic. He dug through an old wooden army footlocker until he found the object of his search, then came down the stairs with a small green book in his hand.

"What is that, Sam?" Mary asked.

"It's a Vietnamese Bible. It looks like after Wednesday, we will never see Lien again. I must try to win her to Christ. I can barely think of her going back to 'Nam. I can't bear the thought of her going to hell."

Sam went off by himself to pray and brush up on the plan of salvation in Vietnamese. When he returned, he sat Lien at the kitchen table and opened the Vietnamese Bible to the third chapter of Romans. Mary watched Lien's face as she listened to Sam and Lien converse in the strange language of the little girl's birth. Lien smiled and nodded when Sam asked her questions. Soon she bowed her head and prayed.

Lien had heard the story of Jesus and His death on the cross many times from her new father. She understood that Jesus loved her and had died for her. Now Sam was asking her to make a decision to trust Jesus as her Savior. She trusted her father, which made it easy for her to trust the Lord.

"Sweetie?" Sam said. "I'm going to give you this Bible to keep for always. I know you don't understand a lot now, but you will. I'm writing some scriptures on the inside cover with today's date. When you see this date and read these verses, you will remember what happened here today."

Lien took the Bible from Sam and held it close to her heart. "I will never forget, my father," she said.

Lien climbed up on Sam's lap and held him close. Mary wiped her eyes and kissed them both on the cheek.

Sam brushed Lien's hair from her eyes and spoke. "We may never see her again down here, Mary, but we will always be together in heaven."

* * *

Late Tuesday evening, Sam explained to Lien that she must go back to Vietnam. She did not understand it all, but she soon became resigned to her fate.

"Sweetie, they tell me that your grandparents and aunts and uncles are waiting for you back in your village. Isn't that good news? They love you very much and want you to come home to them," Sam said, knowing in his heart that his words might not be true. But he had to give her something to hold on to.

"I always love you, my American mother and father. Do not forget Lien," she said with an earnest expression on her little face. She sat between Sam and Mary on the couch, with Brenda and Amberley on the floor. Mary tried not to weep in front of the child, but she could not hold back her tears.

"And remember us, Lien, your American sisters," Brenda said, seated next to Amberley on the floor. "We will never forget you."

The next morning, Lien asked Mary if she might have fried cornmeal mush for her last breakfast. "I will never be able to make fried mush again without thinking of Lien," Mary said to her family as they sat around the kitchen table.

Mary gave Lien a photograph she had made of the whole family together. "This is so you will never forget us, sweetheart," Mary said, putting the photo in Lien's Bible.

At half past ten, a woman from child welfare came for Lien. Amberley and Brenda carried her little suitcase out to the car. They all quickly kissed and hugged her one by one, and Sam buckled her into her seat. Within minutes she was unceremoniously gone out of their lives forever.

Sam went to his pickup truck without looking back and drove off to work. Mary put her arms around her two remaining girls and wept softly.

"I'll never leave you, Ma," Brenda said.

"Nor will I," said Amberley.

Twenty
The Buckles

Thanksgiving came and left softly as the Bridges comforted themselves, trusting that God was in control of everything. They prayed for little Lien and thanked God for bringing her into their lives, if only for a brief moment.

Mary and Grandma Andrews wanted to send Christmas gifts to Lien, but the State Department said it wouldn't be possible for them to further communicate with her in any way.

"The Lord is with her, Mary. We will have to be satisfied with that," Grandma said.

Soon, the December storms came to replace the early snows of November. Billy Gussette quickly got over Lien, and being the fickle eight-year-old he was, fell in love with Brenda all over again.

The weather was unusually snowy and difficult for folks to get out. Mary was especially concerned about Andy and Sarah Buckles, the elderly black couple who lived in Hipps Hollow by the old mill on the river. They were in their seventies and had no other family as far as anyone knew. They lived in an old, one-roomed tar-paper cottage next to the river.

The Buckles were very independent and lived as hermits. They grew a big garden every year, and they canned and dried almost everything they needed, storing it in a large underground root cellar. Andy had dug a small inlet pond with a built-in fish trap on the edge of the river that kept them stocked with live suckers, catfish, and an occasional salmon. Andy also trapped rabbits and squirrels, and he dried and salted the meat for winter. Sarah cleverly made slippers and mittens out of the dried fur and skins, which she sold in town for a few dollars apiece. Sometimes a farmer would bring them a deer or a quarter of beef or half a hog.

The Buckles had a few chickens and a cow for milk and cheese. Their brown Guernsey lived in a lean-to that was almost as large as the tar-paper cottage.

Sam and some of the local farmers checked on the Buckles from time to time. But the weather had been so foul lately that they had been almost forgotten. Andy had told Sam earlier that summer that it was getting harder and harder for them to get about.

Mary loved the Buckles. She had played at their cottage in the woods when she was a little girl and spent many long afternoons helping Sarah with her canning and tending her little patch of mustard greens. Andy had made Mary her own little set of garden tools, and she had diligently worked next to Sarah in her garden. She had learned to sew from Sarah, who patiently helped her make a pair of slippers out of soft rabbit's fur. Mary still had them and kept them carefully preserved in one of her drawers.

"Go check on them, Sam," she said. "I've made them a hot beef stew and biscuits."

Sam loaded a covered basket full of Mary's good cooking into the truck and drove the slippery, narrow road down into the hollow. A plume of smoke was wafting from the chimney, and Sam saw the curtain move at the window. He beeped the horn.

"Andy? Andy Buckles?" he called out.

The door opened with a creak, and Andy stood at the door.

"Why Sam, whut brings ya out here?"

"Mary was worried about you and Sarah and wanted me to check on you. Is everything well?" Sam said, taking the basket of food off the front seat.

"Well, bless yer hearts, Sam. We are doin' fair to middlin', I guess. Come on in."

Sam stepped through the sagging wooden door and was immediately at the table in the center of the room. He set the basket down. "Mary cooked you up some beef stew and some of her buttermilk biscuits."

"Thanks, Sam," Sarah said, getting up from her chair where she was peeling a large rutabaga. "Tell Mary she's a dear."

"Are you folks getting along all right? Do you have enough food and firewood?"

"Food's holdin' out," Andy answered, "but the early snow and cold has made uh big dent in our firewood."

"I'll bring you out some coal. It burns hotter and lasts longer."

"Can't afford ta pay ya, Sam," Andy said. "It shames me to take charity."

Sam folded his arms. "Andy, I once thought like you. I almost put my family in the poorhouse because I didn't want to take any help. Now just let your neighbors lend a hand and don't be so stubborn!"

Andy lowered his head and chuckled. "All right, Sam."

"If I get going now I can be back before it gets dark."

Sam filled his pickup bed from the mountain of coal beside the railroad tracks in Sodus and delivered it to the Buckles. The truck bed sagged from the weight of the coal until the tires rubbed the fender wells.

"I'll sleep a lot better knowing you have plenty of heat, Andy," Sam said.

* * *

Amberley and Brenda were making supper while Ma sat at the table working on her shopping list. Brenda diced an onion and mixed it with dry oatmeal, an egg, spices, and ground beef. Two strips of bacon were put on the bottom of a loaf pan and covered with a sauce made from ketchup, brown sugar, and mustard. The ground beef mixture was then packed on top of the bacon and sauce and put in the oven to bake.

Amberley washed several potatoes and put them in the oven beside the meatloaf.

"We need a green vegetable too, girls," Ma said without looking up from her work.

Amberley and Brenda looked at each other and laughed.

"What's so funny?" Ma asked.

"Nothing, Ma," Amberley said. "It's just that everything seems to come to you so naturally."

"What do you mean by naturally?"

"Well, you're so well organized. Running this house comes as second nature to you. You always seem to know just what to do or say without thinking about it. It all seems so effortless."

Ma smiled. "I appreciate the compliment, girls, but I had to learn everything I know. I made your dad suffer through a lot of concoctions when we first got married." Ma pressed her lips together to stifle a laugh.

"What is it, Ma?" Amberley asked.

"I was just remembering how Grandma Andrews reacted the night I put blue food coloring in her chicken and noodles. She told me I had better get that ring on my finger first before cooking my fiancé his first meal."

"What's all the merriment going on here? I hope it's not at my expense," Dad said as he walked in the back door.

"Hi, Dad!" the girls said as they each scurried to give him a hug and kiss. "Supper's not ready yet."

"I'm in no hurry." Dad walked to the sink and washed the black coal dust from his hands.

"How are Andy and Sarah, Sam?" Ma asked.

"Oh, about as good as could be expected. They're getting old, Mary. I don't know how much longer they can live in the hollow. I took them a load of coal this afternoon."

"Can't the government help them, Dad?" Brenda asked, remembering the monthly trips down to the welfare office with her real father to collect his check.

"Well, honey, I don't think Andy or Sarah have ever worked anywhere. I don't even know if they have social security numbers. You have to pay in to be able to take out. Besides, I think Andy would look upon it as charity."

"Sam, do you suppose they have any kin living nearby?" Ma asked. "I don't remember them having any children."

"I heard somewhere that they have a daughter living out of state, but who knows? I wish we could get them out of that hollow into a decent place," Dad said as he left the kitchen to change his sooty clothes.

"Well, I'm going to fix them up a real nice Christmas basket and take it over on Christmas Eve. Girls, would you like to make them some gifts?" Ma asked.

Amberley spoke first. "Sure, Ma! I have several pairs of slippers I've knitted, and Brenda is almost finished with a quilt she's been working on. Maybe they would like something different than rabbit fur. And say, I'll bet Mrs. Enkins would like to send something along too!"

"I am sure she would," Ma said. "She has always thought kindly of the Buckles and has given us some wonderful Christmases, too." And then Ma sat down at the kitchen table and began drying her eyes with the dish towel she held in her hands. The girls looked soberly at each other.

"It's Lien, isn't it, Ma?" Amberley said softly, putting her hand on Ma's shoulder.

Ma nodded. "In all of this bustle, I almost forgot about her. Oh, where is she now, and what is she doing? How can we have a merry Christmas when we don't know what has happened to her?"

Twenty-One
A Land Without Hope

Lien sat silently in her chair at the airport, watching the huge planes taxi down the runway and then roar off into the sky. It was hot and humid in the islands of the Philippines, and beads of perspiration ran down her little face, for she was still dressed in the clothes she had worn when she left the winter weather in Sodus. Occasionally an official from the airport would check on her, but she was not offered anything to eat or drink or even a word of comfort. She was awaiting the plane from Vietnam that would take her back to the land of her birth, and no one wanted anything to do with her.

Suddenly, a stern voice from behind her spoke in Vietnamese. "Get up, little girl! Take your things with you."

Lien turned around, and there stood a Vietnamese soldier in his uniform, staring down at her as if she was a dog. He did not smile. "Up, daughter of traitor! Let us go now!"

Lien wanted to cry, but she was too afraid. She dragged her suitcase along with both hands and followed the man out the door onto the tarmac. An awaiting jeep took them out to an isolated landing strip where a dark green airplane with Vietnamese government markings was parked. As the little girl struggled to get onto the plane, a crewman jerked the suitcase from her hands, spilling its contents all over the runway. Lien put her hands on her face and began to cry. The crewman uttered a word of disgust as he stuffed everything back into the suitcase and tossed it up into the plane. As he poised to close the door, he noticed a little green book that had fallen from Lien's suitcase.

Lien was horrified. *Oh, it's my Bible, and the photograph that Ma gave me!*

The crewman picked up the book and quickly thumbed through it. Seeing that it was a Bible, he tossed it out onto the runway and slammed the door shut behind him.

* * *

Amberley sat on her bed finishing her homework while Brenda quietly read a book at the blue wicker desk. Brenda loved to read, and Ma had bought her an old book about English history for her birthday. As she flipped through the pages, she noted an old painting of a Saxon warrior. How magnificent he looked—brave in his tunic and coat of mail, holding a javelin and a shield.

Amberley closed her book with a clap, bringing

Brenda back to the twentieth century. The girls readied for bed, and Amberley had her devotions while Brenda listened in. After she prayed, she noticed that Brenda was unusually quiet, staring at the ceiling.

"What is it, sis?" Amberley asked.

"Oh, I was just thinking about little Lien. I can't seem to get her out of my mind."

"Me too. I pray that she'll be all right. Maybe if Vietnam opens up again in a few years, she can come back to us," Amberley said, trying to force a smile.

"Maybe, but from what Dad says, it's almost a land without hope," Brenda said, turning to face the wall.

The house was quiet except for the wind and the tree branch that always seemed to rub against the bedroom window. Amberley could hear the muffled voices of Dad and Ma talking together in the living room. She loved that sound because it made her feel secure. She wondered if Lien had anyone to make her feel that way now.

"Amber," Brenda said after a long silence. "Do you remember when I asked you if prayer ever works?"

"Yeah," Amberley said apprehensively, not sure where Brenda was going with the question.

Brenda paused. "See you in the morning."

Twenty-Two
The Christmas Blizzard

As the blue-gray light of the bitter winter morning shone through the girls' bedroom window, they hurried to dress in the chilly room and descended the stairs to help Ma in the toasty kitchen. Amberley stole a quick look out of the front room window to the east, where she could see the reddish ball of the sun peeking out between the horizon and the heavy gray cloud deck that was fast moving in from the northwest. Then, almost like a wink, the sun disappeared as it was engulfed by the clouds. The vanishing sun reminded Amberley of a line from one of her favorite poems, "Snow-bound" by John Greenleaf Whittier —*It sank from sight before it set.*

Dad had gone to work early, and the girls sat down with Ma to have breakfast. The bitter north wind slammed into their house, and Amberley, startled, spilled maple syrup on the table. The walls and roof creaked in defiance of the storm. She peered out the kitchen window. Everything had disappeared in a dusty white cloud of snow.

Ma sat thoughtfully at the table, watching the steadily worsening storm. Then without a word, she stood up and left the kitchen, returning with a large basket of wrapped Christmas gifts.

"I know Christmas is still a few days away, but the weather is so nasty," Ma complained. "It's supposed to snow heavily until the twenty-sixth or -seventh. I want Andy and Sarah to get these presents and the Christmas dinner I was going to make them." She laid a heavy cloth over the whole basket.

"Your father left me the pickup today so I could get groceries. I think I'll take the food and presents over to the Buckles's place this afternoon."

Amberley and Brenda looked at each other. The wind was howling now, and the roads outside of town were sure to be treacherous.

"Ma, please don't go! Wait for Dad to get home," Amberley pleaded, taking Ma by the hand.

Ma smiled as she reached out to pat Amberley's cheek. "I'll be all right, Amber. Just give me a hand getting this food ready."

Several hours later, Amberley and Brenda helped Ma pack the basket of gifts and the pots and pans of food into the green pickup truck. They struggled against the bitter wind and stinging snow, and once Ma slipped and fell into the steadily accumulating drift by the back door.

"Let one of us go with you, Ma," Amberley said,

holding her mother by the arm with both hands to stop her from getting into the driver's seat. She almost had to shout to be heard over the howling wind.

"Now, girls, stop it!" Ma retorted. "I said I will be just fine! I'll be back in forty-five minutes or so."

Brenda and Amberley watched helplessly as the red taillights of the pickup truck quickly disappeared into a swirling cloud of snow. As the girls turned to go back into the house, they were shocked to see how quickly their footprints had been blasted away by the howling wind.

* * *

Mary nervously drove down Hillandale Road to the dirt road that led to the Buckles's cottage in Hipps Hollow. There were no other tracks to follow, and it was difficult to stay on the road. Gusts of wind forced the truck onto the shoulder as she dodged several mailboxes that seemed to jump out in front of her from nowhere. When she finally arrived, Mary honked her horn, and Andy came out to help her unload her Christmas cargo.

"Thank you, Mary," Sarah said, giving Mary a hug. "But was it wise to come out in this weather? Please be careful going back."

"I wanted you to have these things for Christmas, so I brought them out today," Mary told them. "I didn't quite realize it had gotten so bad. I'd better go."

"You jis be careful, Mary. I haven't seen uh snow like this in twenty years," Andy warned.

Mary waved good-bye, climbed into the truck, and pulled the door closed against the wind. With a groan, the truck proceeded down the long hollow to get onto a paved road. Mary peered through the thickly falling snow. Her tracks were already covered.

It hasn't been ten minutes since I came down this road, she thought.

Just ahead, the road seemed to fork. *I don't remember a fork in this road. Which way do I take?*

But before Mary Bridges could think, the pickup truck struck something hidden under the snow. "Oh, dear!" she cried as she felt the right fender glance off a tree. Mary quickly slammed on her brakes, but the truck seemed only to speed up. It fish-tailed as it slid sideways in the blinding snow.

"Oh Lord, please help me!" Mary shouted, but everything was happening too fast. As she struggled with the steering wheel, she felt a numbing *thud* as the truck slammed into another tree. Then came the sensation of falling as the truck slid backwards over the edge of a deep ravine and crashed into a tree.

Everything was instantly still except for the blowing snow and the tinkling of shattered window glass as it fell in pieces across Mary's lap.

Mary slowly opened her eyes. The cold wind and

snow were blowing in where there had once been a windshield. She looked ahead and could see the headlights pointing straight up the hill into the trees. Mary felt her head throb, and she reached up to touch her forehead. Her fingers were smeared with blood.

What is Sam going to say? she thought as the swirling world of white faded into a mist before her eyes.

* * *

Sam and Mr. Enkins pulled into the alley and almost got stuck in the snowdrift that always formed there from year to year.

"One of these years I'm going to get smart and put up a snow fence," Mr. Enkins said with a chuckle.

Sam waved good-bye to his boss as he quickly stepped to the back door of his house and the warmth of the kitchen. As he stomped his boots on the back porch, he noticed that the pickup truck was gone. He set his black lunch box on the counter, surprised that the girls did not greet him in their usual manner.

"What's wrong, ladies? Where's the pickup?" he said as he hung his coat on the hook behind the door. Amberley and Brenda glanced at each other and then looked at their father with serious looks on their faces.

"Dad?" Amberley began slowly. "Ma went to take food and the presents to Andy and Sarah's, and . . ."

175

"What? In this weather?" Sam said, his voice rising. "How long has she been gone?"

"About two hours or so—we begged her not to go," Amberley said.

"What was she thinking? How could someone so smart do something so dumb?" Sam shouted as he slammed the door shut behind him and ran up the alley to get Mr. Enkins. They quickly drove off in Mr. Enkins's pickup truck through the cloud of white to Buckles Hollow to look for Mary.

Andy and Sarah were visibly upset when they heard that Mary hadn't made it home.

"Let me he'p ya, Sam. I can't bear thinkin' uh Mary bein' out there," Andy said, reaching for his hat and coat on the back of the door.

"Thanks, Andy, but you stay here where it's warm. What's Sarah going to do if something happens to you?" Sam put his hand on Andy's shoulder and bid him good-bye with a look.

Sam and Tom Enkins drove up and down the hollow road. They searched until dark, but they could find no trace of Mary or the green pickup truck. It was snowing and blowing so hard that when they drove north on Evans Road, the crossroad of Pipestone seemed to spring out at them from nowhere. Mr. Enkins slammed on his brakes just seconds before he drove into the ditch on the other side.

"Where could she be? It's as if she just went up in

smoke," Sam said in frustration, hitting his knee with his fist. "I've never really cared about death or danger where I was concerned. I always figured if it happened it happened. But how do I deal with this? Mary is the best thing that ever happened to me. How can I go on if she's . . . ?"

Mr. Enkins cut in. "Now hold on there, Sam. Mary's a smart girl. Maybe she went to a farmer's house until the storm blows over. Let's go back and call the sheriff's department."

* * *

Sheriff Warner quickly organized a posse to make a diligent search of the hollow, but to no avail. Ma and the green pickup were nowhere to be found. Amberley and Brenda were in tears, and Dad paced the floor.

"What was she thinking?" was all that he could say, over and over again.

"It'll be all right, Daddy! I have been praying so hard. It'll be all right," Amberley said, sniffing back tears.

Then, with a face Amberley had not seen on her father in a long time, he seemed to snap.

"Yeah, just like it was all right with little Lien! She's back in the jaws of the murderous Cong, and now your mother's lost in a snowstorm. What'll happen next? Yeah, God's really looking after us and answering our prayers!"

Brenda moved to the corner of the kitchen, shaken.

This was a side of Dad and the Bridges family that she had never seen before.

Amberley held her father tightly. "Please, Daddy, don't talk that way. You know the Lord will do what's right —Ma always says so."

Sam Bridges shook loose his daughter's grip and pulled his coat off the hook by the door.

"Maybe the only thing I know is a bottle!" he said, slamming out the door like the father Amberley had known for most of her life. She paused for a moment in shock and then brushed past Brenda to the living room without a word. Brenda heard her run up the stairs to her room and slam the door.

Brenda sat down at the kitchen table. It was quiet except for the howling wind that seemed to gnaw at every window and door, trying to get in.

I guess I have my answer, Brenda thought. *It appears that God can't be trusted after all!*

Twenty-Three
If God Can't Be Trusted

Lien was ordered by the crewman to sit down and be quiet. He tossed her suitcase on the seat next to her and went forward to tell the pilot that he was ready for takeoff. Lien looked around. The plane was empty except for the Vietnamese soldier who had been mean to her in the airport. He sat across the aisle from her, and she watched him quickly fasten his seat belt and then close his eyes to take a nap. Lien looked at her seat belt and attempted to pull it around her, but she could not get it to lock. She looked at the soldier in despair.

He doesn't care about me, she thought. *Nobody will ever care about me again.*

Lien stared out the window at the tropical sky as she heard the loud engines wind up and felt the plane begin its bumpy ride down the runway. She was not sure if Sodus and the Bridges family had just been a dream. The little green Bible and the photograph inside it were the evidence of their love, and they were lying out on the runway, never to be seen again.

179

Does Jesus not love me? she thought. *Does he not care for little Lien anymore?*

Finally, she could not hold back. She hung her head in despair, wringing her heart out in a torrent of tears.

* * *

Brenda stood looking out the kitchen window. An hour or so had passed, and there still was no news about Ma. She didn't know where Dad was, and Amberley had not come back downstairs. As she looked down, she noticed the candle that Ma had always lighted when Dad was late coming home from work. Brenda had never quite understood why she did it, and she hadn't wanted to intrude by asking. Now, it seemed like the natural thing to do. Brenda set the candle in its holder and lit it. It had a soft golden glow against the frosty window glass.

Who would have thought that I would be the one left in charge at a time like this? Brenda faintly smiled to herself, seeing the irony of it all. She walked into the living room and sat in Ma's chair. She picked up Ma's well-worn Bible and held it tightly against her chest with both arms.

What was it that Ma always said? She tried to remember. *God deals with us according to how we trust Him in times of trouble. Wherever Ma is right now, I'll bet she is still trusting God,* Brenda thought. *She has always been my loving example. If she can trust Him, no matter what, then so can I.*

Brenda closed her eyes and began to pray. *Dear God, I have no one here to talk to but You. I have seen the worst in everyone here tonight. All I have heard since I came to live here is that I must trust You with everything, that I must get saved; and yet, Dad and Amberley, who I looked to as examples, are gone.*

Brenda's eyes began to moisten. *I have come to the conclusion, dear Lord, that If You can't be trusted, then who can? I know that You love me and died for me. If You will forgive me and save me, I'd like very much for You to become my Savior right now.*

* * *

Amberley unburied her face from her pillow and sat up on the edge of her bed. She tried to straighten her hair with her fingers and wiped her tears on her sleeve. She was ashamed and embarrassed, but she could not seem to get a hold of herself.

Dear Lord. She tried to pray, but couldn't. The words seemed thick and heavy like wood. *Perhaps God won't hear me because of the way I am acting,* she thought.

Amberley stood up and glanced at herself in the mirror. She shook her head at the sight of her red eyes and puffy face. She opened the bedroom door slowly and stood at the top of the stairs. Brenda was sitting in Ma's chair, holding her Bible. She had been crying too, for she was drying her tears with a tissue. Amberley quietly walked

181

down the stairs. Brenda stood up as if to speak, but she said nothing as Amberley walked past her into the kitchen and stood in silence in front of the hot oil stove.

Suddenly, overcome with grief, Amberley turned and bolted outside. Hurrying down the alley, she pounded on the Enkins's door. The door quickly opened, and Mr. and Mrs. Enkins were standing there in the bright light of the room.

"Why, Amber!" Mr. Enkins said. "Where is your coat, young lady?"

"Come here, honey," Mrs. Enkins said, noting Amberley's tears. Amberley threw herself into Mrs. Enkins's arms.

"Honey, don't give up hope. I'm sure we will find your ma, and she will be okay," Mrs. Enkins said. "This isn't Canada or the Yukon. Sodus Township is a small place, and we will find her."

"Oh, Mrs. Enkins!" Amberley sobbed. "Dad is so upset about Ma. I'm afraid he's going to start drinking again! He left the house and we don't know where he is."

Brenda came rushing in the back door after her sister. "Amber?" she said.

"Gracious!" Mrs. Enkins exclaimed. "Two young rabbits without their fur!"

"Amber, are you okay?" Brenda asked.

Amberley turned her tear-streaked face to her adopted sister. "Oh, Brenda, first we lost Lien, and now Ma and

182

Dad! What is happening to us? Doesn't God care about us anymore?"

Amberley buried her face in Mrs. Enkins's arms. Tom Enkins grabbed his hat and coat.

"I'll go find Sam," he said.

"There, there, honey," said Mrs. Enkins, patting Amberley on the back. "Let it all out."

Amberley sniffed. "What hurts so badly is that I trusted Him so much—but now this! It's just too hard!"

Brenda spoke up, hesitating at first. "That sounds so strange coming from you, sis. You are the one who taught me that I should trust the Lord." Brenda smiled slightly as though she couldn't believe her own boldness.

Amberley wiped her eyes and stared at Brenda's smile. *I've got to snap out of this,* she thought. *Brenda is cool and calm, and I've fallen to pieces. I am the one who is supposed to be there for her, and now she is comforting me.*

Tom Enkins reappeared and stuck his head in the door. "Girls, you need to come and see this."

Everyone moved quickly to the alley. Coming down the snow-choked street, in and out of the clouds of snow, was a horse-drawn wagon. A single gas lantern lit the way. The wagon turned up the alley, and a heavily bundled voice exclaimed, "Whoa, Pete! You people there—give me uh hand!"

Mr. and Mrs. Enkins and the girls ran to the wagon. Lying under what seemed to be tons of blankets and quilts was Ma. She peered up at them with a smile. Her face was bruised and scratched, but she seemed not to be badly hurt.

"I saw th' headlights from her pickup truck in uh ravine by Buckles Holler. She's all right—jus' shook up," the wagon driver said, stepping down and removing his hat and scarf. There, standing tall in the blowing white, was Joe Schenkle from Shanghai. The bully who had terrorized Billy Gussette and Amberley in the schoolyard. The same bully who had met his match in Brenda.

Joe handed his lantern to Mr. Enkins, picked up Ma from the wagon bed, and carried her inside. He laid her on the couch and covered her up with one of his quilts.

"I feel like such an idiot! What is your father going to say?" Ma said. "I think I destroyed the truck."

"Oh, Ma!" Amberley said. "We were so worried and upset."

Brenda kneeled down next to Ma and held her hand. "Is there anything I can get you? Some hot tea or something?"

"No, sweetie, I'm fine for now," Ma said with a smile. The scratches on her face were purple from the cold, and a bump showed conspicuously on her forehead. "Where's your father?" Ma asked, looking at the girls. Amberley and Brenda glanced at each other.

"Well, Ma," Brenda began.

"Mary?" Mrs. Enkins interrupted. "It's Sam on the phone. He wants to speak with you. He's at Pastor

Mitchell's."

"Girls, help me sit up," Ma said, leaning stiffly on one elbow.

"Now, Ma, lay back down. I can hold the phone for you," Brenda said, taking the receiver from Mrs. Enkins and holding it close to her adopted mother's ear.

"Hello?" Ma said. "Oh, Sam! I did such a stupid thing. I'm so sorry. I think I ruined the pickup truck."

Ma listened on the phone for several minutes, nodding though Dad couldn't see her. She looked so pitiful with her bruises and scratches. As she spoke with Dad, a tear ran down her cheek onto the pillow.

"No, Sam. I won't ever do anything like that again," Ma said. She handed the phone to Brenda when she was finished.

"What did Dad say, Ma?" Amberley asked. "Was he angry?"

"Well, he said that if I ever scared him again like this . . . well, he said he loved me!"

Joe Schenkle had been standing quietly in the shadows at the corner of the room. Ma raised a hand in his direction.

"Thank you, Joe. You saved my life. I don't know what would have happened if you hadn't come along," she said.

"Aw, I was glad ta help." Joe smiled and blushed.

Brenda looked at Joe and suddenly saw a different person standing there. The boy for whom she had felt nothing but contempt and disgust had instantly disappeared, and a noble young man was left in his place. He stood tall in his bib overalls and heavy denim coat. He had a brown plaid blanket draped over his shoulders, and he folded his arms across his chest. His face was handsome, and the bitter wind and biting snow had seemed to have no affect on him. In a strange, wonderful way, he looked like the painting of the Saxon warrior in her book. She walked slowly up to Joe.

"I want to thank you, Joe, for what you did for Ma. You are so brave—and I don't think you are half as tough as you think you are," Brenda said, smiling.

* * *

Amberley sat on the floor next to Brenda, laying her head against Ma's arm. Joe and Mr. and Mrs. Enkins had long gone, and Dad was seated in his favorite chair. Everyone but Amberley was asleep—too tired to go up to bed.

Just an hour or so ago, she had been hysterical with fear and grief over Dad and Ma, and now they were safe and secure in their own home. Amberley seemed to hear the tender words of the Lord speaking to her. *O thou of little faith, wherefore didst thou doubt?*

She now realized that the situation could have gone either way. *Dad might have backslidden, and Ma might have been killed. And after all, Lien is still gone,* she thought. *But does that mean I should stop trusting? I let God down when I failed to trust Him with the outcome—no matter what it was.*

Amberley closed her eyes as a tear escaped down her cheek. *Forgive me,* she prayed. Instantly, she felt a warmth around her—the familiar arms of Jesus holding her, just as they always had when she was a girl. She smiled through her tears.

God had been trustworthy all along. It was only she who had failed to keep her part of the relationship—but now, faithful as always, after teaching her, He had forgiven.

Twenty-Four
A Christmas Gift From Above

The plane was finally airborne, and it circled the runway before launching out over the vast Pacific Ocean. The bright glare from the sun off the water hurt Lien's eyes. She reached into her pocket and pulled out a small plastic bag with several oyster crackers at the bottom. This was all that was left of the little snacks Ma had sent along with her.

As Lien laid her head back and looked out the window again, she was surprised to see a large American military jet pull alongside the plane. It was painted in different shades of green and brown and had a white star on the side. She had seen many like this in Vietnam. It paused for a minute or so outside her window and then darted away.

Suddenly, her plane turned hard, sending her suitcase crashing to the floor and almost knocking her out of her seat. The soldier across the aisle woke up, startled. The crewman came rushing back to where they sat, waving his arms and shouting frantically. An American jet had seen smoke pouring from their plane, and they had to make an emergency landing back at the Philippine airport. As the plane began its descent to the runway, Lien could see several firetrucks below with their red lights flashing. *They are not as pretty as the first firetruck I saw in Grand Rapids,* she thought.

She looked across the aisle where the mighty Vietnamese soldier was squirming nervously in his seat, glancing from window to window in fear. He repeatedly shouted out to the crewman, asking him if they were going to crash.

He is a coward, Lien thought to herself in disgust. *He is only brave when he is bullying little girls.* Lien didn't care if the plane crashed. She didn't want to return to Vietnam.

As the plane taxied to a stop at a remote corner of the airport, the pilot, the soldier, and the crewman quickly unlatched the door and fled out onto the tarmac, leaving Lien alone to her fate. Almost instantly, several large men dressed in firemen's coats boarded the plane and started spraying a fluffy white foam on everything. Soon, the windows and seats and everything else was covered with the thick froth, including Lien. Before she could react in panic or fear, one of the firemen ran up to her. He was an American, but he spoke to her in Vietnamese.

"Lien?" he said. "I want you to trust me. Say absolutely nothing and do exactly as I tell you. Can you do that?" Lien quickly nodded, and with that, the fireman picked up the tiny little girl and put her under his fireman's

189

coat. "Hang onto me with all your might," he whispered.

As the two men backed out of the plane, one of them tossed a small green box down the aisle. Quickly, they ran to the firetruck, and one of the firemen opened a compartment door on the side. He tenderly placed Lien inside and whispered to her in Vietnamese.

"Are you able to be brave?" he asked. Lien nodded again, all covered in foam.

"No matter what happens, you must not make a sound." The fireman smiled and winked at her, and then he closed and latched the door.

The men jumped into the firetruck and sped away to the other end of the runway where the Vietnamese crew stood in bewilderment. Suddenly, the plane off in the distance exploded in a ball of orange and black fire. Everyone watched in amazement, including the Vietnamese. They spoke among themselves of their good fortune to have gotten off the plane before it exploded.

No mention was made of the little girl who, to their knowledge, was still inside.

* * *

The lights from the Christmas tree shone in a sparkling rainbow through the window onto the small, fluffy white lawn. It was Christmas Eve in old Sodus, and everyone was safe inside. The house smelled of roasted peanuts, hot out of the oven, and buttery popcorn. Brenda had made hot chocolate and baked cookies. Boxes and packages of all shapes and sizes littered the floor around the tree.

Ma lay on the couch, still healing from her accident, waited on hand and foot by Sam and the girls. The local radio station, WHFB, softly played "I'll Be Home for Christmas." They quieted as they listened, realizing together that one of them would not be home this year—or ever.

"I've asked the Lord a thousand times to forgive me for not trusting Him. I always thought I had such great faith," Amberley said thoughtfully.

"Well, I found out how easy it is for the sow that was washed to return to her wallowing in the mire," Dad said, setting his coffee cup down.

"If I had used better sense, none of this would have happened. I scared the daylights out of everybody and almost got myself killed. How can I ever tell you all how sorry I am?" Ma said, struggling to sit up. She was still very sore, and she bit her lip to conceal it from everyone.

"Forget it, Mary. It's Christmas now, and we need to let it go. We are all together—for the most part—and that's what's important."

"Brenda?" Ma said, motioning for Brenda to sit next to her. "I am so happy that you finally got saved. Every time I spoke to you about it, you seemed not to be interested.

What changed your mind?"

"Oh, Ma, I was always interested, and I did hear every word you said. I just wasn't ready to trust anybody, including God. But when everything seemed to be falling apart, I realized for the first time that He was the only one who could really be trusted. It was easy after that."

The Bridges sat around the big tree, listening to Bing Crosby sing "White Christmas." Amberley thought she was seeing things when a bright red light flashed on and off through the window of the front room.

"Oh my goodness, what is that, Sam?" Ma said, craning her neck to look. "Not Santa Claus, I hope."

"It appears to be a state police car," Sam said as he stood to look out the front window. "There's a trooper coming up the walk."

He went to open the door.

"Sam Bridges?" the stern-voiced trooper asked.

"I'm Sam Bridges. What can I do for you?"

"I have something for you," the trooper said, handing Sam two envelopes.

"Won't you come in, sir?" Sam asked, swinging the door wide.

"Don't mind if I do," the trooper said, half-smiling to himself as he stepped inside—leaving the door wide open.

Sam opened the first letter, which appeared to be a Christmas card. He read it aloud:

Merry Christmas, Sam, to you and your family!

Signed, Captain Bill Adams and Lieutenant Tim Farlaigh

(formerly) United States Army Special Forces

Sam looked up at the smiling trooper with a look of bewilderment on his face.

"I guess I don't understand," he said.

The trooper grinned as his partner opened the back door of the squad car. There, standing knee-deep in the fluffy snow, was little Lien.

"How?" Sam whispered under his breath as he rushed out the door to meet the little girl.

Lien ran up the snowy steps into his arms as they wept together. The trooper brought in Lien's only bag and handed it to Sam. "Oh, and here's this," he said, handing Sam a little green Vietnamese Bible and bidding him Merry Christmas.

"What is it, Sam? What's all the commotion?" Mary shouted.

"Look what I got for Christmas, girls!" Sam said as he brought Lien into the room.

Amberley and Brenda squealed with joy when they saw her. They ran to her as Lien held out her tiny arms to them. The girls hugged and kissed her and finally placed her into Ma's loving arms. She hugged Lien as she wept and thanked God.

"How, Sam? What does this all mean?"

Sam unfolded and read the several pages of a letter that was enclosed in the Christmas card:

Dear Sam,

As agents for the State Department, we became aware of your problem with Judge Richardson regarding Lien. We personally investigated and were able to get evidence to convince her to change her mind, but it was too late. The Communists had already picked up the little girl. It was an absolute miracle of timing when we were able to get an air force jet to intercept her plane. To make a long story short, we set it up so that a couple of our guys from the Forces could rescue Lien. You would have been proud, Sam. Please don't ask for details, but as far as Vietnam is concerned, Lien doesn't exist anymore. She is out of their world and into yours forever. We apologize for the theatrics, but we thought you wouldn't mind after you saw what we were up to. Merry Christmas and good luck to your good family and your new daughter.

Bill and Tim

P.S. We would appreciate it if you kept this letter to yourself and your family. This might cause a ruckus if it got out. B.A.

194

De Oppresso Liber

Sam handed the letter to Ma. "And here's another letter, Mary. It's from Judge Richardson."

> Dear Mr. and Mrs. Bridges,
> I'm so sorry about all of this, and I assure you that I have tried to move heaven and earth to make it right. Come and see me after the first of the year. I can promise you that I will do everything in my power to help you adopt little Lien Huong.
> Sincerely,
> Emily Richardson

Everyone sat up until midnight watching little Lien sleep softly in Ma's arms. Amberley was scarcely able to take it all in. Just a few days before, she had shown the weakness of her faith and accused the Lord in her heart of letting them down. Now, all the objects of her failed trust were seated warmly and securely in her living room on Christmas Eve.

Amberley looked over at Brenda, who had fallen asleep on the floor next to Ma. Her wonderful strength of character had allowed her to be strong when the family needed her most. Brenda had learned for herself and unintentionally taught them all that one's faith in God is not something you can turn on and off as you would a light

195

switch. Amberley smiled, overwhelmed with love for her sister—and for her other sister, the little one who was now sleeping soundly on Ma's lap.

"Take her up to bed, girls," Ma said.

"No, Mary, I'll carry her up myself," Dad said. "I just want to hold her for a while until I'm sure it's not a dream."

THE END

Recommended Reading

The Amazing Story of Creation from Science and the Bible
Dinosaurs by Design
>   By Duane T. Gish, PhD
>>   Both available from Institute for Creation Research,
>>   www.icr.org

The Little House Cookbook
>   By Barbara M. Walker
>   HarperCollins Publishers
>   www.littlehousebooks.com

The Green Berets
>   By Tom Streissguth
>   Capstone High-Interest Books
>   www.capstonepress.com

www.ingramcontent.com/pod-product-compliance
Lightning Source LLC
Chambersburg PA
CBHW060809120626
46557CB00001B/136